LAST TRAIN TO KINGSTON

Claremary P. Sweeney

Publisher's Information

EBookBakery Books

Author contact: claremarypsweeney@yahoo.com
Author blog: AroundZuzusBarn.com

Photography by the author, Claremary P. Sweeney
Cover by Zachary Perry - ZperryDesigns.com

ISBN 978-1-938517-69-3

1. Mystery. 2. Murder. 3. Claremary Sweeney
4. South County Rhode Island. 5. Kingston Station

LAST TRAIN TO KINGSTON

This book is for Charley, my favorite partner in crime.

Sunday Night, November 15

Thea tugged at the warm, woolen cape, pulling it up around her neck. The chill dampness of the November night mingled with the acrid smell of smoke from a nearby chimney. For a brief moment, she stood alone on the edge of the platform. Her eyes swept across the front of the Victorian wood-framed train station. Not much had changed since she'd left eight years ago. Inside, overhead lights reflected into round yellow puddles on the well-worn oak benches, empty now, as the station master began his routine of closing up for the night.

Stepping away from the lamplight, she walked through the shadows softening the old stationhouse into shades of gray. A lone taxi collected one of the few passengers arriving at this late hour, then drove off toward the main road, its high beams glancing over her.

Thea continued toward the south side of the depot savoring the comfort of the darkness enveloping her. Sensing the uneven ground beneath her feet, she cautiously made her way onto the cement path running parallel to the tracks on the other side of the black wrought-iron fence.

Up ahead there was a slight shifting. Pressing the worn leather brief case closer to her chest, she continued toward the bench at the entrance to the bike path.

Something scurried, followed by a snap and then another, like brittle twigs splitting apart. She gazed into the shadows behind the bench - their bench. An anxious feeling washed over her. No one was there yet to greet her. The parking lot had emptied. Inside, the station house lights switched off.

She looked down. A package was lying on the seat. A gift? She remembered the last time someone had given her a gift - an engagement ring nestled inside the deep purple velvet lining of a small white satin box. But that was decades ago. She stared off into the night hoping to spy someone waiting for her to open the surprise.

To the east, a Leonids Meteor fell across the background of an inky sky. It descended much slower than the Perseids Showers she'd seen when visiting that summer so long ago. Meteors were practically invisible where she lived - too much ambient light in a big city. But in the countryside, if there was no cloud cover, the light spectacle could be seen all night long flashing brightly overhead.

Tonight's moon was a citrine sliver in the vast, black sky. Perfect for watching stars flying through the heavens. Another descended. Closing her eyes, she made a wish. She sat down, dropping the briefcase on the bench, causing the package to topple over. A ring fell out, much larger than the last ring she'd been given. She lifted it to her face and then sniffed. Cherry. A candy ring pop. Someone's idea of a joke, she supposed. She tucked it back inside the box.

A slight breeze rustled the last of the clinging leaves. A dry, clicking sound. The northbound train began to roll along the track, shaking the ground, building up speed. Its whistle blew and then, silence enveloped her. Suddenly, overcome with a deep weariness, she bowed her head.

Gloved fingertips brushed softly along the nape of her neck. Startled, she twisted around. An ominous figure stood towering over her, its arms raised toward the heavens. She gasped, opening her mouth in fright. No scream issued forth to pierce the quiet night. Just a weak protest. A pitiful, cracked, "Nuhhh!" stuck in her throat. Her hands moved protectively to ward against the impending blow. In that brief moment, she glimpsed another star streaking across the sky. And then, darkness.

Lying there, her life slowly ebbing away, Thea murmured one last wish as the warmth of her breath rose and faded into the cool night air. No one heard.

During the day, students walked the two or so miles from the train station to their dorms or to the frat or sorority houses and graduate apartment units lacing the outskirts of the nearby campus. But the last train into Kingston usually held one or two people choosing not to venture along the deserted roadway at that time of night. Not even for such a short distance.

Rick Carnavale looked to the sky as another star flickered and disappeared into the blackness. He'd dropped off his fare and was headed back onto Route 138.

The Sunday concert at the Courthouse Center for the Arts had let out later than usual. Rick turned his cab into the parking lot, pulled up past the side door and waited to see if anyone was left inside who needed a ride. No one signaled to him and when the last few cars had departed, he shut off the motor.

He got out and strode across a walkway of cement slabs. Each one was engraved with the name of a donor who'd contributed funds for restoring the historic courthouse, making it into a community arts and performance center. Stepping back for a moment, he admired the old Romanesque-style, grey-stone building dating back to 1894. "They don't make them like this any more," he stated to himself before climbing the steps leading up to the double-doored entrance.

His voice echoed through the hallway as he called into the darkened rooms on the first floor, "Gino? Hey Gino!" Getting no response, he ascended the wide oak staircase leading to an upstairs theatre, once a busy courtroom for Washington County.

Expecting to find his brother cleaning up after the performance, he discovered that the room was empty. The band had already broken down its equipment and the stage was bare except for a microphone stand, two speakers and some electrical cords.

He began putting the folding chairs away. When he'd almost finished, the sound of a door opening caused him to turn. His brother limped in. He had on Doc Martens, farmer jeans, a brown and green-checked flannel shirt with the sleeves pushed up, its frayed cuffs meeting faded yellow latex gloves that stretched past his elbows.

"Nice look, Gino. Piss yellow is definitely your color. I thought you'd stood me up!"

"Nah. I was just waitin 'til you were done with the chairs. Ya missed a few back there."

Rick laughed. "Your timing's still impeccable. Like when we were kids. Showing up after all the work's done."

"Well, the men's room still needs cleanin'. Maybe I'll go out and come back a little later?" He stripped off the gloves and hurled them at his twin who promptly threw them back at him.

"Sorry 'bout that, Bro. I don't do toilets." Rick held out his hands, "It would ruin my french-tipped manicure. But I'd be glad to help you straighten up the bar. Get rid of a few of those extra beers nobody bought tonight."

"Yeah, I sure could use some help with that," Gino informed him with a chuckle.

They went downstairs. Light from the hall spilled into a room with wooden chairs, round café tables and a small bar at the far end. Rick flipped on the light switch. Paintings by local artists filled the wall space and he proceeded to side step from picture to picture, his eyes surveying each canvas carefully.

"Hey, dis one here's not so bad. I like the look of that old-time steam train coming outta the picture right atcha."

His brother brought two beers to one of the tables and they both took a full swig before they sat down.

"Yeah, I like that one, too. I might buy it to hang in my formal library. I think it'd look real classy over my artfully illustrated, coffee table copy of *The Little Engine That Could,*" Gino quipped. They clanked their bottles together in a brotherly toast.

"To us!"

"Yeah! To us!"

Minutes passed and then Rick broke the silence, "So, you texted that you needed to see me. What can I do for ya?" He sat waiting, watching his brother chug from the amber bottle, fully expecting him to ask for yet another loan. And he'd have given him his entire night's wages without a second thought. But this time Gino surprised him.

Taking an envelope from his pocket, Gino proudly tossed it down and pushed it across the table with a flourish.

Rick slowly opened the flap. He pulled out a thick bundle of crisp hundred dollar bills. He looked up, "You know I don't want anything back."

"Yeah, I know. You never do. You're a real good brother, Rick. And I wancha ta know I appreciate all the help you been given me and Sophia lately when we really needed it. But this afternoon the insurance check came in from my accident claim and I had ta share it with you."

"You sure?"

"Yup. There's plenty left. Just don't say nothin' to the wife. She'd end up spending it all on shoes." He gave his brother a slap on the arm and brought out another wad of money from his pocket. "Tonight, all drinks are on me."

Taking their beers out to the front steps, they sat quietly watching as the white, tapered tail of a falling star streaked through the dark sky.

"What are you gonna wish for, Gino?"

"Nuttin. Not a thing, Rick. Tonight I can truly say I got everything I could ever possibly want."

Monday Morning, November 16

Detective Lieutenant Kara Langley stood in line at Allie's waiting to pay for her coffee and three boxes of donuts she'd bought to bring into the office that morning. Since September, her team had been working over-time to solve a rash of housebreaks in the Moonstone Beach area. They'd finally closed the case just the day before.

It was time to regroup and take a breather after two months of tracking down clues, doing interviews, following leads and filling out tons of paperwork. Now they'd arrested the people involved and could turn the evidence and their case over to the lawyers to let them battle it out. Just in time before Thanksgiving.

She paid the cashier and left the comforting, doughy aroma coming from the small donut shop that had been there on Quaker Lane ever since she could remember. When she was a student at the local university, it was a favorite place for folks to stop in the summer on their way to the South County beaches. She was gingerly positioning the boxes on the back seat of her car when her cell phone rang. It was the dispatcher.

"Hey! Good morning, Leo."

"Lieutenant Langley, the Chief needs you to get over to the train station fast. An early-morning jogger found a body down at the entrance to the bike path."

"Any other info?"

"The guy noticed someone lying on a bench and when he saw the blood, he phoned it in. Two patrolmen are already at the scene and your team should be getting there about now."

"Okay, Leo. I'm on my way."

She arrived ten minutes later to find the area already cordoned off. Police were busy taking photos, being careful not to disturb the crime scene. A sergeant stood off to one side talking quietly to a young man wearing green sweat pants and a light blue t-shirt with URI, her alma mater, in bold navy letters on the front.

"Good Morning, Lieutenant Langley," Sergeant Shwinnard said as she approached them.

Kara nodded. "Not so much for her," she responded, gazing at the body of a woman lying under a black woolen cape. One arm hung down stiffly, the pale fingers not quite touching the ground. Her forehead was gashed. Blood congealed among the thin strands of white hair.

"Detective Langley, this is Jeff Weintraub, the jogger who found her, " Shwinnard said.

She looked at Weintraub, noting the condition of his clothes and running shoes, and held out her hand. His grasp was firm and she felt no bruises or cuts. He blinked as she stared into his eyes.

"Mr. Weintraub, could you tell me what you saw when you arrived?"

The man hesitated and then began his account of arriving in the lot, parking his car and walking to the bench at the entrance to the path.

"Like I told the sergeant, I work nearby. I usually try to run real early and I always stop first to do some warm-ups at the bench." He cleared his throat. "But when I got here this morning, she was just lying there. The thought crossed my mind it might be someone waiting to catch the train. She seemed to be asleep. When I looked more carefully, I realized she wasn't sleeping."

His voice wavered a bit. "I called 911 on my cell. Then I waited over there until the police arrived." He nodded toward the kiosk and the bulletin board displaying maps and information on the William O'Neill Bike Path.

"Mr. Weintraub, was anyone else around?"

"No, not when I first got here. But then people began parking up at the other end of the lot and going into the station."

"We'll need a witness report from you." Kara signaled for a policewoman standing nearby and gave instructions for Weintraub to follow the police car back to the safety complex to make a formal statement.

An officer called out "Lieutenant Langley, we've found something."

She walked toward him through the grasses leading to a gully behind the bench. He pointed to a large rock. "Looks like it was tossed back here. Blood would indicate it was the weapon used. The victim could have been seated and turned as the killer came from behind. There are no other wounds we can see, but we'll have to wait for the medical examiner to confirm."

"Any identification?"

"Nothing so far. We'll check more carefully after Harry's done with her," he said nodding to the parking lot where a black Buick Regal Sedan had just arrived.

Everyone stopped what they were doing. They all knew Harry Henderson's reputation. He was a stickler about people not messing things up before he could do a preliminary examination of the body. Nobody wanted to get on his bad side, especially this early in the day. His tall, lanky form walked briskly past them, kit in hand, mumbling something about "being on call" and "this ungodly hour" under his breath.

"Not much of a morning person," the sergeant commented under his breath as they all moved out of the way to let him do his job. Kara stood by his side as he examined the body.

"Female, Caucasian, looks to be in her seventies. She's been dead a few hours. Appears to have died from a blow to the head, but I'll know more after I do the post-mortem."

"Her seventies?" Kara gazed down at the woman lying on the bench. "She looks like a sleeping child," she said softly. "Thanks, Harry."

She left him to finish up and headed toward the train station. Police were questioning the early morning commuters, but no one had seen anything.

She stopped to confer with one of the officers. "How're we doing here, Detective?"

"I spoke with the station master, Jack Reynolds. He came on duty at around 5:50AM. He says he didn't see anything suspicious. I asked him to run a check on passengers to Kingston. Our victim bought a ticket in New York at Penn Station under the name Dorathea Lorimar. I sent her name to the Chief. Maybe he can get some more info on her."

"Anything would be a help right now," Kara said.

"Reynolds said Roger Timpson was on duty last night. I'm on a town softball team with him. He lives nearby. I'll go and talk to him now if you don't need me here."

KINGSTON STATION

Reynolds was inside the office behind the ticket window announcing the arrival of the northbound train to Boston. Kara knew him. His wife Emma was a friend and a regular volunteer at the Kingston Free Library in the Village.

"Hello, Jack."

"Mornin', Kara. How's it goin'outside?" He nodded in the direction of the bike path.

"The medical examiner's working there now, finishing up. I think we'll be able to move out of the back parking lot area later this morning. We've roped it off for the present. Sorry for the inconvenience, Jack. I know Detective Brown's already spoken with you, but I have a few more questions. I'll wait until you're done."

She took a brochure from the stand just inside the doorway. Sitting on one of the long wooden benches, she studied the schedule.

The room quickly emptied of the last few customers. Reynolds closed the ticket window and opened the office door for Kara to enter. She moved to a stool and sat down.

"You said you got here about 5:50AM. Was anybody hanging around?"

"A car arrived. Dropped a young couple off just as I was opening up. Your sergeant already spoke with them. They were students from the university traveling to Boston for the day, returning later tonight."

"Anybody else?"

"It was still a bit dark, but the outside lights were on and I think I'd have noticed someone waiting around the station. There were cars in the lot. Sometimes they're parked for a week at a time- people going to New York or DC to visit or on business."

"So, nothing unusual?"

"Nope, not that I could see. I opened up the building and people began arriving a while later to catch the southbound train."

"Timpson, the person who did the night shift? The name's familiar. Any relation to Lucille?"

"Her husband. He's been working here for a few months. Nice guy. Really dependable. Lives nearby on Blackbird Street. I gave the detective his address and phone number. Should be home now, probably still asleep."

"You checked the passenger listing and gave Detective Brown the name of a Dorathea Lorimar."

"Yeah, the ticket was purchased in New York at Penn Station."

"Thanks, Jack. If you think of anything else that might be of help to us, call me. Tell Emma I said 'Hi' and I'll see her at book club."

"Will do, Kara."

She went outside. People were getting out of cars and waving goodbye. She had a lot of questions needing answers and this was just the beginning. She wondered if Lorimar was somebody from the area or a visitor? If she was, why take the late train? And who would want to kill her once she arrived in Kingston?

Kara walked over to the team working around the crime scene. It was going to be a long morning for all of them. She knew there were many pieces to this puzzle and it would be their job to fit them together. The biggest piece right now was to find out why Dorathea Lorimar spent her last moments sitting alone on a bench near the bike path in the dead of night.

Darnell Sharkey turned over in his bed. He was still wearing the clothes he'd had on the night before. His mouth was dry, a sour taste under his tongue, and the lids of his pale blue eyes were almost crusted shut. Voices drifted up the stairs. His mother was talking with someone. It sounded like his ex-girlfriend, JayZee.

He sat up suddenly. *That skank has a hell of a nerve coming around here.* One of the guys at the bar had let him know she'd been dating someone else. He got up and went to the bedroom door, trying to catch some of the conversation. What he heard suddenly had him rushing down the stairs and into the kitchen, startling both women.

"Darnell, JayZee came by on her way to work. To pick up her bicycle." Geralynn looked over at the girl who began to inch closer to the door.

"Get outta my house!" he screamed. His greasy, dark brown hair stood on end and his long arms flailed as he lunged toward her like an animal suddenly breaking its chains.

Geralynn didn't budge, crossing her arms and placing her large bulk between them. He grabbed her by the shoulders, but it gave JayZee enough time to get outside. He pushed past his mother into the back yard.

"You don't think I know what you're up to? I heard what you two were talking about. You tell that Nordstrum bitch I'll have her job. I'll come down to that two-bit newspaper and introduce her to my shotgun."

JayZee darted quickly around the house to the front yard with Darnell close behind. Geralynn had tromped through the living room out to the front porch, arriving just as the frightened girl reached her car. Running to the rear of the Chevy, he wrenched the bicycle from its rack and heaved it down on the front lawn.

He stood there shaking his fist at her. "Tell that reporter I'll kill her if she runs that story. And when I'm done with her, I'm comin' to get you, you ugly bitch!"

"Darnell, enough! You don't threaten people in my house," his mother's voice shook with anger.

"Your house?" He turned, his irate face damp with sweat, saliva spewing from his chapped lips. "You wouldn't even have this house except for me! This is my house! My house!"

Geralynn clutched at her chest. JayZee leapt from the car and started back to help her.

"I'm all right, JayZee. Just go!"

The girl hesitated, then bolted back into the car, locking the door. She kept her eyes on the mother and son as she turned on the ignition and drove away from the house.

Geralynn waited until she was safely gone and then sat down heavily on the rocker trying to catch her breath. She watched as a furious Darnell kicked at the back tire of JayZee's bicycle and began stomping on it.

When he'd finished, he came up on the porch, glaring down at his mother as he yanked open the screen door.

She said in a low voice, almost a whisper, "You pack up your stuff and get out of this house."

He started to object, but one look at her flushed face silenced him. "Pack your bags, Darnell, and get out. Now!"

Neeka peered out the front parlor window as Samuel crossed the street. She rapped on the glass pane and waved to her neighbor. He'd just finished changing the flat tire on her car and was headed for home.

Monday was her usual day off and Neeka Nordstrum had things to do. Picking up Arthur's set of car keys from the counter, she realized she'd have to get a better hiding place for them if she didn't want to end up back at the police station. Arthur had been stopped and warned on multiple occasions. Driving was now out of the question.

His car had been pulled over twice traveling erratically on Kingstown Road and last week, for the third time, he was brought into the station.

He'd appeared to be very disoriented and kept insisting he had to get to the bank. They called her at work.

When she arrived, he was remanded into her custody and she was advised to take away his keys. Her friend, Lieutenant Langley, told her, "He can't be allowed out on the road again for his own good."

Arthur's driving days were over and the resulting loss of independence was devastating to him. Each time he was reminded his license had been revoked was a reawakening of disappointment and a sharp sting of betrayal.

Yesterday morning, he'd refused to leave his bedroom. Neeka knew he eventually would forget why he was angry and come out to eat. She'd made a large meatloaf, wrapped it in aluminum foil and placed it in the refrigerator to be reheated for dinner. He loved meatloaf and gravy and mashed potatoes and mushy peas. He could have that meal every night of the week.

She checked on him. He was sleeping soundly. Returning upstairs to her bedroom and opening her closet, she picked out the day's outfit: a silky, cornflower blue dress with elbow-length, cuffed sleeves. The soft material draped and fell perfectly over her trim figure. The v-shaped neckline showed a bit of bare cleavage, her golden skin highlighting the delicate sapphire pendant dangling on a silver chain. She chose a fitted, navy jacket and matching shoes to add a professional touch to the ensemble. Tiny sterling silver earrings shaped like starfish sparkled as she brushed her short-cropped, auburn hair to a lustrous sheen.

Looking into the mirror, she applied a thin line of black mascara to emphasize her violet-colored eyes. She coyly batted her lashes to check the effect and flashed a brilliant smile at the thirty-five year-old woman who, in her opinion, appeared to be much, much younger.

The cell phone on the night table began to play the shark music from *Jaws*. It was her boss. She thought about ignoring it. Lavinia was a pain in the butt. It never seemed to occur to her editor that there was life outside of the newspaper for the poor minions working under her. As she answered the phone, Neeka wondered if the woman ever left the comfort of her cushy office to actually cover a story herself.

"Hey, Vinnie, what's up?"

"Sorry to bother you on your day off, but I need someone down at the train station. It appears there's been a murder."

"Where's Justin?"

"He called in. Says he's really sick. I think he's just paranoid. Says someone spiked his drinks last night. Look, you're close by. Could you go over there as soon as possible and report back to me? I'll send one of the photographers to get some shots."

"Will do." Standing at attention, Neeka saluted the phone.

She went downstairs, checking once more on the old man before she left the house. A twinge of excitement came over her. She hadn't covered a murder in years - not since her days on *The Connecticut Current.* This could very well be the news story she'd been waiting for to make her famous.

Within five minutes, she arrived at the crime scene. The young policeman guarding the parking lot gave her a long, appreciative look. She pulled out her ID then put it back into her bag when he told her not to bother, he knew who she was. She'd covered a previous case and he recognized her. She gave him her brightest smile and he gave her what little information could be released. No identification had been found on the body and the area was still being searched for evidence. Statements were being taken.

She spied Kara coming from the station house and went to meet her. The two women made for a striking contrast in the early morning light. Although they were about the same height, Neeka seemed to be a pale, thin wisp standing next to the detective lieutenant's solid presence.

Kara also was dressed in blue; a practical navy skirt and jacket with pockets that were large enough to hold things meant for a small handbag. Her light aqua blouse sported no frills but served to accent the dark brown face and deep-set hazel eyes now focused on her friend.

"Hey, Kara."

"Morning, Neeka. So, you're on this case?"

"Yup. Justin had too much to drink last night. I had to throw his bike in my car and drive him home. But that means I finally get to cover something other than planning board meetings. Look, Mike just filled me in. Is there anything else you can tell me?"

"Not yet. We'll be working on this for a while."

"Do you think the victim came in on the train?"

"We're checking on that. Not much to go on right now." Kara quickly changed the subject. "I saw Arthur at the Kingston Hill Book Store the other day. He didn't have much to say."

"He's been acting a bit testy lately, adjusting to not being allowed to drive. He's still furious about getting stopped and brought into the station last week. With the dementia, I'm sure he'll soon forget all about it."

"So, he's been to a doctor and diagnosed with dementia?"

"Just last month, but I've been noticing him slowly deteriorating over the past year."

"It must be tough to see him this way."

"It is. I remember being awed when I first met him - this brilliant author living right here in Kingston. It's really sad to see him trying to navigate through everyday routines, but he has some good days and that's a blessing. I'm there to do what I can to make it easier on him."

"Are you staying at his house or your apartment?"

"Most evenings I'm at his place. I do some cleaning up and make us something for dinner. He's usually in bed by seven, but lately he's been getting up and roaming around. I've hidden the car keys, like you said. Apparently, though, he found them last night because they were on the kitchen counter this morning. I'll take them with me from now on. Um, I think your sergeant is trying to get your attention."

"Okay, see you around."

"Call me if you find out something more I can use for the paper?"

Neeka returned to the site and spoke with the photographer. "Doug, could you get some shots of the area around the bench and the bike path?"

"Sure Neeka. I took some good ones of the police working the scene and the front of the building. Any idea who the victim was?"

"Not yet. Hopefully, there'll be a report when I stop by the police station later today."

She called in to the office, "Hi, Vin. Not much to go on yet, but I'll be there in about twenty minutes with what I've got. Doug will be coming in with the pictures as soon as he's done here."

Before she tucked it back into her bag, she used her cell phone to take a photo of the bench, thinking how peaceful it seemed in the soft morning light. This certainly didn't look like a place where a brutal murder had been committed, but she wasn't naïve and she knew that murder could happen anywhere, any time.

❧

Earlier, he'd heard the back door slam shut and Neeka's car starting up. Arthur listened as the tires rolled over the gravel drive and then he fell back into a fitful sleep for another hour.

When he woke again, his head was throbbing. Opening his eyes, he tried to collect his thoughts. He knew he was at home, but something seemed strange to him.

Carefully placing one foot and then the other on the floor, he slowly began to push himself off the bed. He stepped into his corduroy slippers. It was chilly in the house. Neeka must have forgotten to turn the heat up before she left. He put on his robe and shuffled to the kitchen.

On the table were a spoon and bowl, a glass of prune juice, a small pitcher of milk and a box of cereal. He picked it up and read the front of the package. His favorite, he thought, and then he wasn't so sure. Turning it around, he read the back of the box. He sat down, poured the milk in the bowl and added the cereal. Lifting a spoonful to his mouth, he chewed and swallowed. Eventually, he began the whole process again.

"Yes, indeed, *Fruit Loops*. My favorite," he said out loud to himself, slurping up the milk and smacking his lips. He sniffed the glass of prune juice and wrinkled his nose in disgust. Getting up from the table, he looked around the room. It was beginning to seem familiar to him. This was a good sign, he thought.

Shuffling back into the bedroom, he started to get dressed in the clothes he'd worn the previous day. As he buttoned the fleeced-lined flannel shirt jacket, he noticed something on the left cuff. Examining it closer, he sniffed. It smelled like blood. There was a small gash on the palm of his hand. He didn't remember cutting himself, but he'd been helping his friend Sam with some yard work on Sunday, putting the rose bushes to bed for the winter. It may have happened then.

Taking the shirt off, he threw it on the floor of the closet and reached up for one hanging where Neeka had placed it on Saturday when she put the clean laundry away. Slipping into his loafers, he stood thinking about what he needed to do today. First thing on the agenda was to find his car keys. He just had to remember where he'd put them. After that he had to get to the bank, although he wasn't sure why. He'd been absent-minded lately. More and more he'd found his things in the strangest places.

Sighing, he began his search, taking the lid from the cookie jar and feeling around inside. He snatched up the lone Oreo and popped it into his mouth. He remembered finding them in the freezer once, although he couldn't imagine what had possessed him to place his keys in the refrigerator.

He removed the ice cube trays, examined them and put them on the counter. Taking out the two remaining ice cream sandwiches, he sat back down at the table, unwrapped both and licked the cool, vanilla filling from along the sides. For a while he was distracted by thoughts of how much he loved ice cream sandwiches. The soft, chocolate, chewy outside layers and the smooth, creamy vanilla filling. He'd instructed Neeka not to buy the crunchy kind. Or the peppermint ones. When he'd finished eating, his mind meandered for a time until finally, he remembered his quest.

Standing in the den in front of the shelf holding the few books he owned, he searched for the missing keys thinking he may have tucked them safely in among his favorite writers: J.D. Salinger, Harper Lee, and Emily Dickinson. He felt a kinship with them. They'd all lived in small towns and valued their privacy.

He reached up and touched the spine of the leather-bound copy of *A Quiet Death* – the book that had changed his life forever. He removed it from the shelf and cradled it. This was his, the novel that had taken him from life as a nobody to that of a famous, beloved author. He gently caressed the embossed title with the tips of his fingers, like a father touching his baby's face for the first time.

A tune came into his thoughts. Familiar and comforting. He sat down in the rocker and began to hum it, cradling the book against his chest. It was a lullaby. The one used in the opening scenes of the film version of his book. The company, which had bought the rights, had been scrupulously careful to keep as close as possible to the text. People loved the movie, probably even more than the book itself. It had made him rich, with money still pouring in.

But he chose to live simply and had no use for material things. What he wanted could never be bought. This thought caused tears to well up in his eyes, trickling down his cheeks and onto the cover. He sat for the longest time until sunlight streamed into the room.

He rose unsteadily from the chair. Bringing his book back to the shelf, he tucked it into the empty space. He'd decided to give up looking for his keys and take a walk around the village. Something had been gnawing at him for quite a long time and he needed to talk with someone. Someone who would understand. Someone he could trust.

Monday Afternoon, November 16

Kara had her team fanning out around the area behind the crime scene. She took Sergeant Shwinnard and two of the younger officers to the bike path in search of anything that looked out of place. Dark clouds loomed overhead. Sunlight intermittently broke through, speckling the black asphalt and the surrounding wooded area.

They'd spent much of the morning speaking to the people working in the businesses abutting the path and interviewing the neighbors living in the houses near the train station. Now, they were concentrating on searching the woodlands and swamp bordering it. A pair of squirrels chased each other on the ground and then up into the tall oaks a few yards from the bench where the body had been found.

The officers walked along carefully scanning the surroundings.

"Detective Langley?"

"Yes?"

"I've found something over here in the leaves. An envelope. Nothing inside, but it's stained. Could be blood. It hasn't been here long."

He pointed it out to her and she bent down to take a look. It was a tan, manila envelope, no writing or printing. Empty, although it obviously had once been sealed. A jagged section had been pulled from the adhesive strip.

"Let's get some photos, Sergeant. I'll check around this area more carefully."

A few feet away, she spied something glinting in the dappled, afternoon light. Bright Christmas tinsel hanging from a bush. She reached out and plucked it from the branch. Beneath it, her eye caught sight of a receipt, the ink blurred by the morning dew. "Get some pictures of this, too."

When he was done, Kara carefully picked it up and bagged it. They continued down the path until reaching the bridge where she peered over the rails to get a glimpse of the fairy houses children said were hidden among the reeds below. They'd walked less than a mile. Up ahead, the path crossed Ministerial Road, well-known for the mountain laurel lining the roadside in early summer. Kara sent the two officers further on. She instructed her sergeant to drive around and pick them up in the patrol car where the path eventually intersected South Road.

"I'll meet you back at the station. Right now, I'm going to see if I can talk with the taxi driver on duty last night."

She returned to the parking lot. Passing by the crime scene, Kara stopped once again at the bench. In the distance, a train whistle severed the calm afternoon air.

Fall was Kara's favorite time of year. Although the bike path was quiet today, come Saturday and Sunday, the crowds would converge. Bikers, joggers, walkers, and baby strollers all sharing the final weeks before the icy cold and snow set in. The last two winters had been brutal in Rhode Island and people were trying to get the most out of these waning autumn days.

South County slowed down in the winter. Tourists were long gone and the pace became a leisurely one. Locals could safely emerge from their houses on to the main roads leading into the little towns of Peace Dale and Wakefield without being caught up in a jam of beach traffic. The aisles of Belmont's Food Market filled with locals shopping and chatting. Circling the lot in search of a coveted parking space was a thing of the not-so-distant summer time.

In neighboring Kingston, professors, students and staff lined up after each class session to make their way onto Route 138. They waited patiently in their idling cars on Lower or Upper College Road for a break in the traffic flow. Locals were well aware of these intervals during the day and took measures to avoid getting caught up in it.

Students usually disappeared on weekends, leaving a hush to descend on the campus and its surrounding area. By mid-November, the town had comfortably settled into its post-tourist/returning college students routine when everyone could enjoy the change of seasons before winter arrived.

Kara had graduated from the university and after getting a job and spending more than seven years on the New York City Police Force, she came back to settle in where she felt most at home. She loved South County and now couldn't imagine ever living anywhere else.

Cases like this tore into the core of a quiet community. A violent murder intruded on the serenity inherent in many small New England towns. She was determined to find the person who caused this rent in the fabric of calm which normally enveloped them all.

❧

Neeka tapped on the door of Lavinia Bloom's office.

"Come in," a husky, smoker's voice called to her.

She gave a little curtsy before opening the door.

"Hello, Vinnie." She placed a printout on the desk. "Here's the article. I interviewed the jogger who found the murder victim and I got some quotes from the daytime stationmaster. He wouldn't give me any names from the passenger list but Roger Timpson was on duty last night. I spoke with him and he remembered a white truck parked outside the entrance during his shift and he saw a taxi leaving around the time he started closing up. It's not much, but it's the best I can do right now."

Lavinia read the article. "Follow-up on that truck and get hold of the taxi driver. Keep on your sources. Hopefully we'll get more information before we go to press on Wednesday. Something's bound to come to light."

"I'm heading home early to check on Arthur. I heard him roaming around late last night when I went to bed, but he was sound asleep this morning. The car keys were left on the kitchen counter but his Camry was still stored safely in the garage. He couldn't have gone anywhere because when I got home around ten, I noticed a tire was almost flat on my car. It was parked in the driveway all night."

"Better start hiding those keys before he hurts himself or someone else."

"I thought I'd figured out a good place under the ice cube trays, but he must've had a craving for ice cream. I found some wrappers on the counter. I've got the keys in my bag, so I know he can't go far today."

She returned to her desk to finish a small article she'd been working on and then phoned Justin.

"Hey, it's Neeka. How're you feeling?"

"Not so great. My head's still spinning and I can't keep anything down."

"You weren't doing so well when I dropped you off last night."

"Thanks for the ride home. Something must've been wrong with my drinks. I don't get it. You drank way more than me, and I'm the one with the massive hangover."

"I stuck around for a while to make sure you were going to be okay."

"I don't remember any of that, but I appreciate it anyway. I spent most of today in bed."

"Too, bad! Lots happening. There was a murder this morning at the train station."

"Whoa! Who's covering it?"

"Vinnie asked me to."

"Was the victim local?"

"There was no ID on the body. I did some interviews and Doug took a few shots, but I'll have to wait for the rest of the info when the police release a report."

"Did Leo have anything for you?"

"Not yet, but he's a pretty dependable source. I'll be by to see you after I'm done here. Do you want me to pick up something for your dinner?"

"No, I think I'll stay away from food for today. But could you bring me some aspirin? I only have a couple left."

"Will do. See you later."

She called the police station. After trying to talk with a detective about the case and being told they were releasing no information at that time, she phoned the dispatcher's cell.

"Leo, can you give me some information on this murder? Everyone seems to be pretty tight-lipped."

"It's crazy around here, and I can't talk right now. I'll call you back when I'm finished my shift."

Her phone rang a half hour later just as she was leaving the office.

"Neeka, it's Leo. There's no official report yet. I don't have much but the victim's name is Dorathea Lorimar. She lives in New York City. Nothing is being released to the public until they can contact the next of kin, so keep it under wraps."

When she arrived at Justin's, he was lying on the couch.

"I got you some aspirin and my buddy at the pharmacy slipped me some oxycodone in case you need something stronger."

"Thanks, Neeka. You look great. I can't believe I'm sick and you're not. You were drinking me under the table last night. Can you stay for a while?"

"I'm going to Arthur's now. Just gotta warm up some meatloaf for his dinner. I'd invite you over, but it doesn't look like you're ready to eat anything, yet. Oh, before I forget, I left your bike in the hall last night. If you don't feel up to taking it to work tomorrow, I can give you a lift on my way in."

"Thanks a lot. I owe you one."

"Hey, consider the debt repaid. If you'd been in the office this morning, I wouldn't be covering the best case we've had in years. Maybe ever. So, thank you!"

❧

It had been a busy afternoon strolling around the village and he needed a quiet place to think. No one ever went up to the second floor of Fayerweather House, so Arthur pushed the curtain aside, climbed the rickety, old, wooden staircase, and went into a attic room filled with the leftover detritus of many years.

He found his usual quiet spot on a faded green horsehaired couch in the corner behind an artificial Christmas tree, assorted floor lamps and shades, a worm-holed desk and some broken chairs.

Bundling his jacket up into a pillow and placing it under his head, he closed his eyes and listened to the sound of someone in the rooms below giving a visitor's tour.

"This two-story, wooden house was constructed in 1820 around a massive stone chimney and was the home of the village blacksmith, George Fayerweather, grandson of a freed slave. He lived here with his wife and twelve children and later his son Soloman took over as smithy. This was an important job in rural communities. Not only did they repair iron, copper and brass items, they also crafted guns, tools and nails.

In 1965 the Kingston Improvement Association acquired and restored the property. Since 1966 it's served as home for the Fayerweather Craft Guild and the Kingston Hill Gardeners...."

The voice faded in and out as Arthur began to nod off and within a few minutes, he'd fallen into a deep sleep.

The brass bell jingled as Neeka opened the back door into the main room. Fayerweather House was abuzz with crafters setting up their wares for Thanksgiving and the Christmas Season ahead. Someone had made popcorn in the microwave and the buttery scent permeated the rooms.

"Hi, Neeka. Don't tell me you're starting your Christmas shopping early this year?" The woman behind the desk was folding white tissue paper on the counter.

"Hello, Cynthia. Nope. I'll probably keep to my typical last minute shopping routine. Why spoil a good thing?"

"I'll be here with Betty on Christmas Eve Day, so we'll make sure we put some things aside for you. What brings you here?"

"I'm looking for Arthur. Have you seen him around?"

"I haven't. Has anyone seen Arthur today?" she asked the people setting up their crafts.

A voice from the kitchenette called out, "He was on the back patio earlier with Samuel." The woman came through the doorway with a fresh bowl of popcorn and offered some to Neeka. "They sat out there on the stone wall for the longest while, just talking."

"Thanks, Betty." Neeka took a handful of the buttered mix. "Did you happen to notice where they went?"

"Not really."

"I think I'll just go next store and see if he's at Sam's."

Betty placed the bowl on the counter. "Is everything okay with Arthur?"

"Not really. He's been a bit distracted lately and I've had to take the car keys away from him."

"That must be tough on him. He loves his independence," Cynthia commented.

"He's been stopped one too many times. The police are worried he'll hurt himself or somebody else and I'm the bad guy who has to enforce the rules."

She chatted a bit and then left through the back door walking across the patio and the grass to the opening between the old stonewall separating the two properties.

Samuel Hazard lived next door. He was a Fayerweather descendant on his mother's side of the family and he still kept a careful watch over the old homestead which was now on the National Register of Historic Places.

He was up on a ladder clearing the gutters of fallen leaves. He stopped working when he heard her call his name. "Hello, Sam. Do you happen to know where Arthur is?"

"I was with him earlier today. He should be home by now. Just a sec, I'm comin' down. I'll finish this later." He moved swiftly and was by her side in a few seconds.

"Thanks for fixing my tire this morning. Sorry I called so early. I noticed it last night when I came in at ten, but I knew you'd probably be in bed already."

"I hit the sack around nine thirty but I'm usually up by five. No problem."

"I'm glad you work farmer's hours. I really needed my car this morning. Vinnie called just after you'd left. She asked me to cover a story. A murder at the train station."

"We don't have many murders in this town. Do you know anything, yet?"

"Not much to go on so far, but the police established the victim wasn't from here."

"A tourist?"

"Nothing on her so far. Sam, would you have any idea where Arthur could be right now?"

"Like I said, he came by and we visited a bit. Then I had some work to do at Fayerweather, so we walked over there and sat on the patio. He said he had something important to tell me but he kept drifting off. He couldn't remember what it was he wanted to say. I don't think he looks well. He needs to see a doctor."

"I took him for his check-up in September."

"What's going on?"

"The doctor diagnosed him with dementia. I've been keeping a close watch on him. I left him sleeping this morning. I was just at the house and he's not there. No note, nothing. I can't find him. Do you know where he went after you talked?"

"Said he was tired and was going to take a nap."

"Maybe he's walking around the village. I'll check in at the book store. Thanks, Sam."

At the end of the path, she turned to look back. He was still watching her as she gave a small wave and started down the brick sidewalk.

Rick Carnavale was raking up leaves in the front yard of his small cottage on Kingstown Road. He heard a car door slam. An attractive black woman came striding across the lawn, walked around a pile of leaves and stood facing him. Although he towered over her, she was not what he'd call petite. She came to his shoulder and that would make her about five feet eight. The way she stood there, jaw set, arms folded across her chest, feet solidly planted in his newly mowed grass, he realized this was not a woman you wanted to tangle with.

Kara took note of the sweeping glance and gave him a quick once over in return. She saw a tall, robust man in his early fifties. It appeared as though he'd spent the summer out in the sun, his skinned deeply tanned.

Taking out a clean white handkerchief to wipe the sweat from his face, he dabbed at his neatly trimmed mustache. She took out her badge and held it up for him to see. He ran his fingers through glistening black hair, pushing it back from his forehead. He was wearing jeans, a long-sleeved orange T-shirt, canvass garden gloves and a Paw Sox baseball cap.

"Detective Kara Langley. We're investigating a murder and I'd like to ask you a few questions about last night."

His thick, black eyebrows jutted up. "Murder? Last night?"

Kara quickly determined Carnavale preferred asking the questions rather than answering them. She was used to dealing with the old Yanks who'd been living here in South County since the dawn of time. She just had to ask the right questions and be persistent.

"You drive the cab that services the train station, is that correct?"

"Yeah."

"Were you driving your cab last night, Mr. Carnavale?"

"Yeah."

"About what time did your shift start?"

"Three."

"And when did you pick up your last fare?"

"When the last train came in."

"And when was that?"

"About 11:55."

"Where did you drop him off?"

"Up on 138."

"Where on 138?"

"Grad apartments."

"Could you tell me which apartment?"

"Number 23. I waited until she was safe inside before I took off."

Ah, he wants me to know he's a knight in shining armor, she thought to herself.

"Where did you go after that, Mr. Carnavale?"

"Arts Center."

"The Courthouse Center for the Arts?"

"Yeah."

"Why did you go there, Mr. Carnavale?"

"The Beaver Brown Band was playing. The concert ran over. I noticed people leaving when I drove by, so I came back to see if anyone needed a ride."

Whoa, three complete sentences!

"And did you get any takers?"

"Nope."

So much for complete sentences.

"Where did you go after that?"

"Inside."

"Inside?" *She could play the same game.*

"Yeah."

"Why?" *At this rate, I may not make it home in time for dinner tonight!*

"My brother's the janitor."

"Your brother's the janitor?" *I'm getting damn good at this!*

"Yeah, he cleans up. I sometimes stop by after a show to help him."

Two whole sentences! "Did you do that last night?"

"Yeah."

"Mr. Carnavale, did you notice anything when you left the train station?"

"A few cars leaving the lot."

"Was anyone hanging around?"

"The station master."

"Besides the station master?"

"Nope."

"Did you see anyone along the road?"

"Nope."

"Thank you Mr. Carnavale. You've been most helpful. Here's my card. Please call if you remember anything. We may ask you to come to the station at some time if we have further questions. Could you give me your brother's name and address?"

"Gino Carnavale. He lives on 138 in the house next to the Center."

Kara left Rick Carnavale to return to raking his leaves. When she got to the car, she glanced back. He was still standing there, leaning on his rake, watching her.

Maybe Sir Galahad wants to make sure I get inside safely?

She thought it really strange that he wasn't the least bit curious about who was murdered or where it happened. Very strange, indeed. She called the station. Detective Sullivan answered.

"So how did you make out with the taxi driver?"

"You mean, Chatty Cathy? I've gotten more information out of a New York street mime! See what you can find out on him for me. I'll be there in a few minutes."

❧

Arthur woke from his nap, stretched, yawned, stood up and put his jacket back on. The aroma of buttered popcorn drifted up to the attic reminding him he was hungry and there was a meatloaf in the fridge waiting for him back home. He went down the staircase and out the front door. He walked along the brick sidewalk across from the bookstore and carefully crossed the street.

He let himself in the back door and hung his hat on the coat tree. The kitchen was a bit chilly, so he turned up the heat and then opened the refrigerator. Unwrapping the leftovers from last night's meal, he covered the meatloaf in ketchup, and ate it cold.

Then he went to the den and turned on the TV. It was too early for the news, so he muted the sound and lay down on the couch.

When Neeka returned to the house, she found him sound asleep, still in his jacket. She cleaned up the kitchen table, placed the ice cube trays back into the freezer, then phoned Kara, but no one answered. She didn't leave a message.

❧

Monday Night, November 16

Kara looked at her caller ID and didn't bother to answer. She'd been chatting comfortably with her best friend, trying to catch up on all that had happened during the time Ruth had spent in England.

When she'd stopped by with an anniversary present and a bottle of Dom Perignon, Kara had exclaimed, "You always remember!"

"Of course I do! I was your maid of honor and it's my fault you're together in the first place,"

"Yes it is. If you hadn't played matchmaker, our stars never would have crossed."

"Oh, I really believe you two would've met at some point in time. This is a very small town and besides, you were made for each other! It was Kismet."

They heard Stewart's car pulling into the garage and Kara checked the roast in the oven.

"Are you sure you won't stay, Ruth? There's plenty of food."

"No way. I have no intention of being a third wheel on your fifth anniversary. It should be shared over a romantic meal with French champagne and don't forget the music! Anyway, I've got a date."

"Someone I know?"

"Arthur and I are going out for dinner. It's his turn to get the check."

Stewart came into the kitchen with a colorful bouquet of mixed fall flowers, which he presented to his wife. She rewarded him with a warm kiss and lingered for a moment, head pressed against his chest listening to his heartbeat.

"Ah, URI's own Neil deGrasse Tyson," Ruth smiled as she threw her old friend a compliment, comparing him to his favorite astrophysicist. "How goes the science department?"

"All's well on campus. We've missed you, Ruth."

"Thanks, Stewart. Cambridge was great but I missed everyone, too. I'm glad to be back and getting things ready for next term."

"I hear there's been some changes in the liberal arts curriculum. What does that mean for your courses?"

"We can talk about that some other time. I'll probably see you at lunch in the Faculty Center some time this week. I'll leave you two star-crossed lovers to celebrate your anniversary. I hear your wife's been busy, so you probably haven't had much alone time, lately. Enjoy the evening."

"Thank you, Ruth. And now I'm going upstairs to change into more comfortable clothes. If you'll excuse me, ladies."

They looked at each other in astonishment. Stewart always dressed in the same outfit: tan Dockers, a woolen flannel, long-sleeved shirt in winter; cotton, short-sleeve, button-down in warmer months; boat shoes, no socks. What could possibly be more comfortable?

"So you're going to eat in your robe and slippers?" Kara called after him.

"I'll surprise you," he said with a chuckle.

After he'd left, they continued their conversation while Ruth put on her jacket to leave.

"Are you still planning on covering Arthur's book in your Modern American Writers' Course?"

"I am. We need to discuss his visiting my class at some point, so the students can ask him questions. He's always avoided it in the past, but I'm going to get him to commit this time."

"You know he hasn't been well?"

"The last time we spoke, he was a bit groggy. Is something else going on?"

"Memory loss, erratic behavior, drowsiness. Neeka tells me he sleeps much of the day away, but roams the house late at night. I've stopped him in his car on Kingstown Road, weaving back and forth over the center line. I told Neeka to take his keys away."

"So, she's still around?"

"Yes, and she's going to be moving in with him eventually. He's been needing more care."

"That's interesting, I didn't get the impression he was that bad." Ruth commented as she opened the door to leave. "Don't forget, we're doing Thanksgiving at my place. I have someone special I want you to meet."

"I'm looking forward to it." Kara blew her friend a kiss as she left.

Stewart returned in the same Dockers but with a different woolen shirt and slippers. He put his arms around her, giving her a big hug. "How was your day? Did they appreciate the donuts?"

She reluctantly pulled herself away from the warmth of his body and began to arrange the flowers in a Waterford Crystal vase they'd received as a wedding present.

"They did when they finally got around to them. We were all called out to the train station. I'm surprised you didn't hear about it on the radio."

"I worked on correcting tests and mid-term papers today and had my CDs on listening to Pink Floyd all the way home. So, I've been out of touch. What's up?"

Together they set the table in the dining room as she told him of the day's events.

"Any idea who the victim is?"

"Her prints were in the system. Dorathea Lorimar. She'd been arrested for a hit and run here in South Kingstown back in 2007. The case was settled out of court and the charges were later dropped."

"So, she's a local?"

"No, her home address was listed at West Fifty-Sixth Street in New York City. I'll be going there this week. No more talk about cop business right now. How was your day?"

"Really great. I received word about that grant for a new telescope and it's looking good. We're in the final heat."

"All that paper work could end up being worth it! Good for you. How were your classes?"

"The Best & Brightest were not happy with my surprise quiz, I can tell you. But I've corrected most of them and it looks like they all did well."

"Ah, your freshmen class isn't so bad after all."

"Well, there were a couple of clueless students who got Astrology mixed up with Astronomy, but they just stopped coming when it got too hard for them."

"Any stars in the class? Forgive the pun."

"Actually, there's one young woman who handed in her term paper early. It's quite interesting and very well written." He opened his brief case and rummaged through some pages, pulling one out and handing it to her.

Kara looked at the paper in her hand and read the title, "'There are More Things in Heaven and on Earth, Horatio…' From Hamlet? The title seems a bit ambiguous for a serious science paper."

"I thought so, too, at first glance. It has a literary tone to it, but the facts are well-researched."

"Maybe she's in one of Ruth's classes? Those were my favorite classes when I was a student. Once, Neeka handed in a paper on Hamlet when we had Ruth for Shakespeare in our sophomore year. Only it wasn't hers. She was dating a senior and he gave her one of his old papers. Unfortunately he'd written it for Ruth's class. I guess he thought Ruth wouldn't remember it and besides, Neeka was only supposed to use it for a reference."

"Did she get caught?"

"Oh, yes she did! Ruth flunked her."

"For the paper?"

"For the course. Neeka thought it wasn't fair because she had straight A's and it was just one paper. And she argued that everyone did it, so it was no big deal. That made Ruth even more resolved. She wouldn't budge. Neeka failed and Ruth said she hoped it would teach her a lesson about cheating."

"I'd say Neeka was lucky that was her only consequence. Plagiarizing's serious business. If somebody pulled that in my class, I'd have turned them in."

"When Neeka came back to Kingston and got friendly with Arthur, it made for some uncomfortable situations."

"Remind me not to invite both of them to a dinner party."

"When would you be throwing a party? Oh, on the same topic - Ruth invited us to Thanksgiving Dinner at her place. I have a funny feeling she plans on introducing us to her newest beau."

"Well, I'll certainly put on my best clothes, then."

"And which of your flannel shirts do you consider your 'best'?"

They both laughed. He kissed the top of her forehead. They opened Ruth's gift.

"Ah, perfect for our Fifth." She placed the set of hand-carved wooden spoons in the salad bowl. The timer on the stove went off. "Pop the champagne, dinner will be on the table in a few minutes."

Soft music came from the CD player as Kara lit the candles in the dining room and dimmed the lights. Stewart handed her a champagne glass. "A toast to us. And to Ruth, who made this all possible."

"Here's to all of us!"

"Happy Anniversary, Honey. Love you!"

"Love you more!"

❧

Neeka tried one more time to reach Kara and then she called Kingston Pizza and ordered a large pepperoni with mushrooms, peppers, and extra cheese. Arthur said he wasn't very hungry and she was not in the mood to cook for herself this evening.

She usually loved working in the large, old-fashioned kitchen. It was such a pleasant change from the kitchenette in her studio apartment. She planned on moving in permanently the following January. It was inevitable. He was on the decline and changes had to be made to ensure his safety and comfort.

He'd hired her to help around the house and over the course of four years she'd gone from a position of part-time help to the role of surrogate daughter. He was not a difficult man to get along with and they shared many of the same interests.

Both were avid readers and many a pleasant evening was spent discussing literature. Although he didn't have many books in the house, he enjoyed visiting the town libraries. And he was always in the Kingston Hill Store buying used books, which he later recycled by giving them back for any charity sales that were taking place.

They'd first met in the basement of the Peace Dale Library soon after she'd severed her ties with *The Connecticut Current* and returned to Rhode Island. They were both rummaging through the mystery book section of the ongoing used-book sale and they chose the exact same one at the exact same moment. He graciously allowed her to walk away with the copy. She spent the afternoon under the oak tree on the front lawn reading P. D. James' *An Unsuitable Job for a Woman.*

They'd had their next encounter the following week on the second floor of the Kingston Free Library during the Annual Village Fair. Once again they found themselves at the mystery book table. He looked at her and said, "Are you following me?" They both laughed at the suggestion and he asked if she'd like to go across the street and join him for lunch. "The Congregational Church is selling hot dogs, soda and chips. I think we can find an empty dining space along the stone wall."

They sat eating their meal, sharing a bag of chips, and talking about what had led them to be here at this place in time.

She'd been hired at a major newspaper in Connecticut right after graduating from URI. She'd hoped the young man who had interviewed her would see to it that she was given assignments in keeping with her talents. But, unfortunately, she'd over-estimated his powers and so Neeka begrudgingly took on the tasks of those who had already crept up beyond the bottom wrung of the novice reporter.

"I did lots of ad copy and obituaries. I worked myself up the ladder from doing book reviews and some special features to helping cover a murder investigation once. That was interesting. And then, a few months ago, I got a chance to work here in South Kingstown and I just decided to come back."

She chose not to share with him what actually had led up to her decision to leave *The Current.*

The owner of the newspaper, a very wealthy widow, happened to come upon Neeka in her office late one night with the young man who'd done that first interview. She'd found them in extremely indiscreet circumstances. The indiscretion might have been overlooked had he not been the newspaper owner's son and heir to the family's fortune. He'd recently married the daughter of a very influential state politician. The union was beneficial on many levels for both families thus, it was mutually agreed upon that the attractive, female interloper had to be sent on her way.

Lawyers handled all of the details and Neeka was laid off with a generous severance package and some extremely impressive reference letters, citing her ability to work well with administration.

Arthur confided in Neeka that he'd grown up in a small midwest town, the son of two librarians. He'd spent much of his early years reading the classics. "My parents decided to home-school me soon after I'd been sent home, clothes tattered, nose bloodied and knees scraped from my first encounter with children not of a bookish nature. This was fine with me. I really didn't like being with other people and I still prefer the characters in books to their real-life counterparts."

"So, how did you end up here in Rhode Island?"

"I got here by way of New York. You see, I'd written some poems and a few short stories. My father entered one of my poems in a contest and I won. A cash prize. My mother was convinced I was brilliant, so she put together an anthology of my writings and sent it to a friend of hers from college who worked for a publishing company in New York. She thought my work was refreshing. One of the stories won me a prize in a writing contest. My book was edited and sent to print. It sold relatively well, so they gave me a small advance and I ended up writing two more books for them."

"Were they published?"

"Yes, and one of them became quite popular."

"Did you live in New York?"

"I stayed in the city for a while but my mother died and I went back home to be with my father. He remarried a few years later and about that time URI asked me to come out to speak at one of their summer conferences. I took the offer and ended up staying."

"Did you ever consider moving back to New York?"

"No, never. In the end, I hated it there. Kingston suits me just fine. It's quiet, I've got a few close friends and other people pretty much leave me alone."

Like Neeka, Arthur was not forthcoming about the incidents leading him away from The Big Apple. He didn't mention that his second book, *A Quiet Death*, became a best seller and won the Pulitzer Prize the following year.

His parents had traveled to New York to celebrate with him but they never made it to the dinner. His mother was struck down by a taxi outside Penn Station.

After her death, Arthur remained in the city for a few months but he eventually returned home, heart-broken by the experience. He didn't share that information with his new friend until a few years later when they had become closer and he looked upon her as a daughter.

Arthur and Neeka sat companionably together on that June day, the sound of an organ concert coming from the open windows of the Kingston Congregational Church. It promised to be the start of a beautiful friendship.

❧

Ruth arrived at the same time as the pizza delivery guy. Neeka opened the door to find her old English professor standing ramrod straight on the stoop waiting to be let in.

It brought back the vivid memory of that day she'd stood in her office. Ruth was a formidable presence even as a young teaching assistant with her sleek, blond hair tied back in a long braid; those bright, green eyes looking accusingly at Neeka and handing her the only paper she'd ever failed.

The woman hadn't changed much in the years following. She waited while the deliveryman took his money and left.

"Dr. Eddleman, hello. I didn't realize you were back from Cambridge," she managed to blurt out as the older woman moved past her through the door and on into the kitchen.

"I've been busy getting settled in and preparing courses for next semester."

Ruth turned to watch as Neeka placed the pizza box on the counter. There was an iciness in the room. Neither chose to carry on the pretense of being friends, although they always maintained an air of civility when they met.

"Is Arthur here?"

"He's in the den. I think he's asleep. He hasn't been well lately."

"I heard he's been having some problems. I'll just see if he still feels like going out."

"Out? It's much too late for him to be going anywhere."

"We made plans," Ruth informed her as she walked into the den where Arthur was lying on the couch.

She stood over him for a minute and then bent down. "Arthur? It's Ruth." Her fingertips gently brushed the wispy white hair from his forehead. "Arthur?"

He opened his eyes. "Ruth, it's good to see you. What are you doing here?"

"You called and invited me out to dinner, remember? Do you still want to go?"

Arthur slowly rose from the couch and blinked a few times. "My head's a little foggy, but I'd love to go out for awhile. Give me time to get ready. Where are we going?"

"I was thinking The Mews."

"Sounds fine to me. I'll just comb my hair and spiff up a bit and I'll be good as new."

The waiter brought them to a booth next to a tree trunk coming up through the floorboards. It had been there for years. The old, grey bark was marked with initials of young lovers who'd had their first date under that tree.

"I'd like a large cheeseburger with the works please. Oh, and I'd like a Narragansett beer," Arthur informed the waiter.

Ruth ordered a pot of tea and fish and chips, explaining that the habits she'd picked up in England were hard to shake off.

"I haven't been to a restaurant in ages." Arthur looked around the room smiling and waving at a baby in a high chair across from them. The waiter returned to the table with their drinks. "I'm glad they're making Gansett again." He took a big swig. "Ummm, that's good."

Ruth chuckled. "There's no accounting for some people's taste. We'll have to stop at the liquor store on the way home and get you a six-pack."

"Sounds like a great idea to me. Can we go by Kentucky Fried Chicken? I'd like to bring a bucket home with me. If I get the large one, it'll last me a couple days."

"Sure. Is there any other place you need to go?"

"No, that'll be fine. I appreciate it. You know, I really miss being able to drive. I never went far, but it was nice to have the freedom to drive into town whenever I felt like it."

"It must be a big change for you, Arthur."

"It is. But I wouldn't want to ever hurt anyone. That would be terrible. A friend of mine had an accident once and she never drove again."

"Arthur. When I left for England, you seemed fine. When did all of this start?"

"I don't really remember. But it's been a few months."

"Have you seen a doctor?"

"Oh, yes. Neeka took me to one at South County Hospital and he did some tests."

"Did he do a Lyme titer test?"

"I'm not sure. Why?"

"Well, this sleepiness. It reminds me of something that happened to me a few years back. I'd been bitten by a deer tick while cleaning up the woods around my house after a storm. Lots of tree limbs had fallen. Remember it? We had no electricity for five days."

"I do remember that."

"Well, I found a rash behind my knee, so I went to a Medical Walk-In Clinic and they took some blood. Come to find out, I had Lyme Disease."

"Lime? Like the fruit?"

"No, like in Lyme, Connecticut where the disease was first discovered."

"So what did you do?"

"Well, they put me on two antibiotics and I felt much better within a couple of days. I still keep a watch on it, though, because it can stay in your system for years."

"You felt better that quickly?"

"I did. Arthur, I'm not saying that's your problem, but I'd like you to get a blood test. Just in case. I could take you over tomorrow morning, if you'd like. And then we could go into Wickford and walk around the town. Maybe have lunch, if you feel up to it?"

"Sounds like a plan."

The waiter arrived with their dinner. "Can I get something else for you?"

"Another Gansett, please," Arthur said.

As they ate, the two old friends caught up on the last year. Arthur loved listening to her stories about Cambridge.

"I wish I had more to tell you, Ruth, but these past few months have been pretty much of a blur for me. I've been doing a lot of reading, though."

"Arthur, I wanted to talk to you about something. I'm placing *A Quiet Death* on next semester's reading list. It's going to be the 50th Anniversary of its publishing and I would love you to come to my class and speak with the students."

"Ruth, I really don't know about that. I just don't think I can do it."

"Okay, but let's see what happens at the doctor's tomorrow. Maybe you'll feel better and we can discuss this again at another time?"

It was late when they drove into the driveway. As she walked her old friend up the porch, Ruth noticed a light in the upstairs bedroom turn off. She knew that Neeka was probably looking down at them as they climbed the steps together and said goodnight. Ruth waited until Arthur was safely inside and turned to leave when the porch light went out.

❧

Tuesday Morning, November 17

Kara was awakened in the early morning hours by the sound of her cell phone.

"Hello."

"Lieutenant, it's Chief Lewis. Sorry to call so early, but I wanted to give you the latest on our murder victim. We've been in touch with the New York City Police where she lived and the Precinct Captain would like to meet with you today. It's going to be really busy in the next week dealing with security for the parade and the tree lighting, so he'd like to take care of this as soon as possible. I said we'd be sending you down this morning. He'll have an officer waiting at Penn Station. He's obtained a search warrant for Lorimar's apartment."

It was a little after 5:00 AM, so she had plenty of time to get things together. "Sure Chief. Who's the main contact?"

"It's someone you worked with when you were in New York. Come down to the station and I'll fill you in."

"I'll be there in an hour."

Stewart turned onto his stomach and threw his arm over her. "So what's up?"

"I guess I'm going to New York sooner than I expected. Promise not to get into any mischief without me?"

"Whoa, you're the one headed for the big city, Little Missy," he twanged.

"Ah, your John Wayne impression! Maybe you should work on that while I'm gone!"

"Gittin' a mite persnickety for a Little Lady!"

"This Little Lady carries a big gun. I'd be careful about all that macho bravado, Cowboy!" She pulled aside the blanket and slapped his butt.

"Hey, it's mighty cold out there, Ma'am! How about we light a campfire under the covers?"

"I'll take a rain check, Pilgrim. Right now I've got a job to do. I'll call when I know more. I'm not sure what time I'll be home tonight. But just in case, stay away from those dance hall gals down at the saloon, Cowboy." She gave him a kiss and pulled the covers over his head. "Love ya!"

"I love you more."

Kara entered the warmth of the waiting room at the Kingston Train Station and went up to the window.

"Mornin' Jack. One round trip to Penn Station."

"Hey, Kara. Headed into New York for a shopping spree?" He held out the receipt.

She knew he was looking for some information about the murder. "I won't be doing any shopping until this case is closed. It could end up being a very lean Christmas for Stewart."

"More motivation to find out who done it fast," he commented.

"If only it were that easy, Jack. Thanks."

She took her receipt, grabbed a copy of the Amtrak schedule and went out the back door.

A few people waiting for the northbound train to Boston acknowledged her with nods or "Good mornings".

Walking along to the elevator, which would take passengers up to the bridge over the tracks to the southbound trains, she looked around. Here she was, returning to New York where she'd worked right after college. It had been an interesting time in her life but the pace had been fast and it had not been as much fun and romantic as she'd imagined it would be. The novelty wore off quickly. Moving back to South Kingstown had felt right at the time.

She enjoyed her life in South County. She really would have preferred staying in Kingston today. Going to work, meeting friends for lunch in town, coming home to a quiet evening with Stewart or going out on one of their weekly date nights to a folk concert at the old Courthouse or a basketball game at URI's Ryan Center. Taking a train to New York City was not what she wanted to be doing.

She settled herself in and began to review the file of information that had been compiled on Dorathea Lorimar. It was sparse. But eight years ago the murder victim had been involved in an accident causing her to be entered in their system. Kara read the report.

Driving along Ministerial Road one night in August of 2007, Lorimar stated she'd heard a bump in the back of her car. She thought she'd run over a tree limb and kept driving. In fact, a bicyclist had grazed the back of her car. He was found sitting dazed on the side of the road by another motorist who stopped and thinking the boy was high, called Emergency 911.

The car Lorimar had been driving was taken to a local shop to repair the damage on the back fender and the mechanic noticed dried blood and notified the police. Lorimar was brought to the station, fingerprinted and released on bail.

It never went to trial and was settled outside of court. The bicyclist's lawyer knew his case was weak due to the fact that it was the teenager, Darnell Sharkey, who had actually run into Lorimar's car. He'd been with friends and was on his way home from a drinking party, peddling fast, not paying attention.

Lorimar had been very concerned and most cooperative when she had found out what had happened. The settlement was generous, covering all of the boy's medical expenses and allowing his mother, Geralynn Sharkey, to buy a house in town.

Kara recognized the name and address. She made a note to meet with the woman when she returned from New York. Settling back in her seat, Kara watched from the window as the countryside rolled on by.

Neeka set a box of cereal and a glass of juice out on the table for Arthur. She'd heard him come in late from his dinner with Ruth the previous night. He'd roamed around for a while and at some point fallen asleep on the couch in the study. She threw a blanket over him, turned up the heat and left to have breakfast with the young woman she was interviewing for her feature article.

As a reporter, she'd covered a few domestic violence cases during her years on *The Current*, but this was to be an in-depth story. She'd been following three local women during the past few months. All had experienced abuse at the hands of their partners. All had been abused as children. Presently, she was tying up some of the loose ends and was almost ready to publish the first installment.

JayZee was waiting for her in a booth at Phil's, a small restaurant in town.

"Hi, Neeka."

"Hi, JayZee." She leaned over to hug her, noticing the girl seemed even thinner than the last time they'd met. She slid into the other side of the booth.

A waitress came to the table with menus and poured a steaming cup of fresh roasted coffee for each of them. The aroma of bacon, sausages, home fries and scrambled eggs wafted over to their booth from the grill directly behind the counter.

The waitress took a pencil from behind her ear and pulled a note pad from her apron pocket. "What can I get for you two this morning?"

JayZee lifted her cup, blowing on the steam rising over the rim to cool it down a bit before taking a sip. "Just the coffee, thanks."

"She'll have a veggie omelet and bring me my usual, Liz. A breakfast sandwich with bacon." The waitress left to place the order.

JayZee took a piece of her hair and began to suck on it. "I'm not really hungry, Neeka."

"You need to eat more. You're shrinking down to nothing. What've you been doing to keep yourself busy?"

JayZee was a quiet, guarded person and Neeka encouraged her to keep up her end of the conversation by constantly asking questions.

"I've been staying with friends, finishing papers, studying for exams and working extra hours at the nursing home."

"If you need someone to study with, just call."

"I'll see my schedule today and get back to you, okay?"

"Sounds good. I'm going to be moving into Arthur's place full time, so maybe you could plan on having dinner with us some night next week?"

"Are you giving up your apartment?"

"The lease runs out at the end of December, so I'll have it until then."

"I may be looking for another place to stay. Maybe I could afford it?"

"It's only a studio and not expensive, so just tell me and I'll put in a good word for you with the landlord."

The twenty-year-old continued to play with her hair, making tiny ringlets with her thumb and index finger.

"JayZee, is everything Okay? You seem anxious."

The girl brushed back her long bangs and looked at Neeka, her pale gold eyes blinking nervously. "I stopped by Geralynn's yesterday morning. I told her you were almost ready to publish the article. She warned me he's been getting worse. Acting like his father used to. Staying out late, coming home drunk. It's like something's set him off again."

"Has he been violent?"

"He came in while I was there. I'm sure he heard us talking. He rushed into the kitchen real mad and when he saw me, that got him going. He was yelling about the article and threatening what he'd do if it got published. He said he'd kill you first and then me. He says he has a gun."

"You don't plan on going back, do you?"

"No, I only stopped by to pick up my bike and visit with Geralynn. I like her. Darnell and I haven't dated in months. I think he has someone else."

The girl paused a moment. "Geralynn told me he came home Sunday night kicking and yelling. She said it wasn't the first time he came home mad. Last week he was throwing things around one day and when she told him to stop, he pushed into her and ran out of the house. She fell down."

"Did she call the police?"

"She warned him she was going to, but she didn't. He took off in his truck. She told me she wasn't really hurt cuz she landed on her butt and it'd made a good cushion. She thought it was just an accident, no real harm done. But with her heart condition, I'm afraid for her. Her blood pressure's been off the charts since he's started up again. She was clutching at her chest when Darnell was chasing after me this morning, but when I tried to help her, she told me to get going. I figured if I left, maybe he'd calm down."

"What does her doctor say?"

"Doctor Gruber put her on another medicine, Norpace, and told her not to skip dosages - to make sure she takes it every day. He's worried, too. I told her I'd pick up her prescription at the pharmacy and drop it off today."

"I don't think you should go back there. I've brought her her medicine before. I'll get it and drop it off when I stop by tomorrow. I've got to see her about something else. I'll talk to her about filing a report on that son of hers. She should get a restraining order."

"I doubt if she'll do it. I think she's worried they'll lock him up."

"Maybe he should be locked up, JayZee?"

"But he was pretty good for a long while. He had a steady job at the golf course, stopped drinking, lost some weight. He really seemed to have it together. But something happened in the past month or so. He started coming in drunk, got fired from the golf course, started being abusive. Just like my dad."

"This sounds dangerous, JayZee. He's lost control. Does he know where you're staying?"

"He knows all my friends, so he could figure it out if he wanted to."

"Why don't you plan on sleeping at the apartment for the next month? The rent's paid for, anyways, and I won't be there much."

"Thanks, Neeka. I'll think about it."

They talked a little about the article and then their food came and they ate. When they were done, Neeka watched as JayZee slipped into her jacket. She turned to give a small wave as she left the restaurant. The bell over the door rang out her departure.

Neeka paid the check and drove down the street to her office. She had a gnawing feeling this was one story that was not going to have a happy ending unless something was done soon.

❧

He was still fuming. His own mother had turned on him. Threw him out! "Bitch, bitch, bitches!"

Darnell slammed the door of his pick-up truck and reached into the back for his duffel bag. He closed the garage and went inside to the mudroom. The house was at the end of a long drive and sat on a hill next to the Usquepaug River.

He'd been taking care of it for the owner, Rusty Russell, a nice old guy he'd met at the Road House Bar in Richmond. He'd hired Darnell to do some odd jobs around the place. Stuff he couldn't manage any more. When Rusty decided to go to Florida for the winter, he told Darnell he could stay there and he'd pay him to keep an eye on the place to make sure the pipes didn't freeze up like last year. This was so much better than his crummy little room at his mother's house.

His mother's house? He wanted to break something! That house should be his. In his name. Was she the one hit by the car? Was she the one scarred for life? A shit life full of problems. No. He was the one. Not her! Nag, nag, nag. "Make your bed, clean up your room, don't leave your dirty dishes on the coffee table." He should be able to leave things wherever he damned well pleased. She should be the one thankful to him for providing her a roof over her head

He knew what they were both up to. He'd overheard them talking. That reporter, Nordstrum, was doing a story making him out to be a pathetic loser. He'd sue the paper and that reporter if they ever printed it. That's what he'd do. If he didn't kill them all first. He'd take care of them all right. He'd show that Nordstrum bitch who was boss. He'd show them all!

Darnell went into the kitchen and opened the heavy cellar door. The lock was tricky, so he propped the door with a brick to make sure it didn't close shut on him. Reaching along the kitchen wall, he found the switch. Lights came on, illuminating the room below.

There were two separate areas dug out underneath the house and the walls of the back room were lined with gun cabinets. He rubbed his hands together. He was looking at his own personal arsenal if he could just figure out where the keys were kept.

&

Tuesday Afternoon, November 17

Gino had been up since the crack of dawn. He'd promised Sophia he'd fix the skylight. She'd decided to make an art studio in the attic and informed him she wanted the natural light to filter in while she created her latest masterpieces.

Rick saw his brother up on the roof during one of his trips along Rte.138 to the train station. He parked in the Courthouse Center's lot and walked across the yard up to the ladder leaning against the house.

Gino was seated with his back resting against the chimney. He shouted, "Hey" and signaled for Rick to come and join him. Rick hated heights, but climbed up, concentrating on making his way over to the chimney without once looking down.

"Make yourself comfortable!" Gino patted a place by his side. Rick cautiously turned to sit facing the road with his shoulders propped against the brickwork.

"Gino, what the hell are you doing up here? You wanna end up in the hospital again? You could fall and bust your head!"

"I'm gettin' a tan."

"It's November, Gino! Geeze, you could do that in one of those tanning booth contraptions at the strip mall."

"Yeah, but they don't let ya bring in a coolah of booze." Gino twisted around to reach inside a small cooler and take out a beer for his brother.

"No thanks. I'm working and when I'm working, I don't drink and drive!"

"Dat's a real good motto. You should sell it to the Department of Transportation. They could make you their poster boy." Gino took a swig from the bottle. "I been watchin' you comin' and goin'."

"It's been busy, so, I figured I'd make some extra dough. Some kind of event going on at the college. How long you been up here?"

"All mornin', pretty much. Sophia wants me to fix this skylight so's she can do her painting in the attic."

"What's wrong with it?"

"It don't open all the way. I cleaned it up real good, so maybe that'll make her happy. It's comin' on winter. I figure she won't need to open it 'til spring and by then she'll probably be doing her art work in one of the other rooms. There's plenty of other rooms we don't even use."

"Makes perfect sense to me." They sat quietly looking down at the traffic watching as a police car entered the parking lot of the Arts Center and then turned and headed back out on to the road.

Rick broke the silence. "Say, Gino, did the cops stop by and ask you any questions about that murder at the train station the other night?"

"Yeah. They were questioning everyone around here to see if any of us knew the woman. Dorothy something. I told 'em I never heard of her and didn't see anything strange goin' on cuz I was working inside at the concert all night. I told them you showed up to help me and left later on. They musta wanted to talk to you on accounta you were doing the late night taxi run."

"A lady cop asked me a bunch of questions. I told her I didn't see anything either. I picked up a fare in front of the station, took her where she asked, left her off and came here. I didn't go near the back of the parking lot where that woman was found. They checked with the kid I dropped off and she confirmed what I'd said."

"The cop wanted me to give her times. I told her I couldn't be sure exactly when you got here, but you showed up around midnight was all I could tell her. Did they ask what you did afterwards?"

"Yeah, I told them I was with you helping clean up. I said it was around midnight, too."

"It don't look like they got any leads. You hear anything around town?"

"Only that it was an older woman who took the train in from New York."

"Imagine that. You leave a nutty place like New York and come here to rural Kingston to get yourself killed on a park bench. I hated the city when we lived there. Filthy, noisy place. Ya know, it's a crazy world. I don't think we're safe anywheres anymore."

"I was thinking the same thing myself, Gino. And now I gotta go. Are you comin' down?"

"No way. The minute she sees my feet on the ground, Sophia'll have somethin' else for me to do. I got enough beer to last me 'til the sun sets. I'm just fine where I am, thank you!"

"Okay. Look, I have tomorrow night off. How about taking in a basketball game? URI's playing Brown and I got a couple of free tickets from a friend."

"Sure, sounds good. Sophia's got her book club and there's nothin' goin' on at the Center, so I'd just be hangin' around."

"I'll come by about six and we can grab a bite before the tip off. That is if you don't kill yourself first."

"Hey, I'm safer up here than you are down there. It's a dangerous world, Bro. Be careful. I only got one brother, ya know."

He watched as Rick slowly inched down the ladder. When he'd reached the bottom, they waved to each other and Gino called out, "Stay safe!"

"You can count on it," Rick yelled back.

❧

The police car had been waiting for her outside Penn Station. It was a warm day for mid-November and the city streets were filled with people coming and going. Sergeant Perez, Kara's old partner, was there to greet her and he took her backpack and tossed it into the back seat.

She settled in as they rode down 8th Avenue in the midst of mid day traffic. Cab drivers and delivery trucks were blaring their horns and the ongoing war of pedestrians and bicyclists versus vehicles was in full swing. She felt no pangs of regret for leaving this teeming hub of perpetual commotion.

They stopped at the precinct station two blocks away from Lorimar's apartment and she spoke with the Captain. He gave her the search warrant they'd need. She and Sergeant Perez decided to walk to West Fifty-Sixth Street.

The outside of the building was quite striking - red brick with well-tended window boxes already filled with winter greens and red and white berries. A middle-aged doorman dressed smartly in a navy blue uniform with red piping around the cuffs and collar opened the front door. They showed their identification and Perez handed him the warrant.

"Yes, I got a call. I was expecting you. My name's Dominic Zimmerman and if you need anything, just tell me. I'll be glad to help in any way I can. I liked Miss Lorimar a lot."

He led them up to the second floor, unlocking the door and escorting them into the entry. "Will you be needing me?"

"I think we'll look around the apartment first. We'll probably want to ask you some questions later, Mr. Zimmerman."

"Please call me Dominic."

"Dominic, what was your impression of Miss Lorimar?"

"She was such a quiet, reserved woman. Kept mostly to herself in this apartment. We hardly ever spoke, but she always had a smile for me. I'm sorry I'll never see her again." He shook his head. "I'll be downstairs in the lobby."

They moved directly into the large living room. Floor-to-ceiling bookcases surrounded them, relieved only by curtainless double windows looking out to the street below, books stacked on its ledge.

A worn leather couch and chair were positioned in front of the windows. There were no mirrors, no knicknacks, no artwork, no photographs to be seen anywhere. Just rows upon rows of books. Kara could have been in the middle of a bookstore for the lack of personal adornment in the room.

At one end of the far wall, a moving ladder, the kind seen in old libraries, reached up to the highest shelf. An archway led into another room also lined with bookshelves filled to the brim. A mahogany desk and black leather barrister's chair sat in the middle of the room.

A smaller arch led into a back room with a twin-sized bed, a night table and a bureau. More bookcases filled the walls. Bifold doors opened to reveal the only closet in the apartment and a single door led into a bathroom with a sink basin, toilet and shower stall. There were no bookcases in the bathroom, only a table stacked with old copies of *The*

Paris Review. The bedroom closet held two identical pairs of brown wool slacks, three blouses in various shades of cream, and brown oxfords. On the shelf above were more books.

"Wow, this lady sure did a lot of reading!" Perez commented.

"That she did," Kara said as she returned to the living room and walked around getting a feel for the place. Books were piled on the floor in front of the bookcases except for one area. Something caught her eye and she gave the wall a shove. The bookshelf wall shifted on an axis and she found herself gazing into the kitchenette on the other side. "Clever! I was wondering if this woman ever ate."

She moved into the tiny space that held some apartment-size appliances and little else. Inside the refrigerator were an apple, an unopened package of English muffins, three eggs, a jar of instant coffee and a carton of orange juice. The open shelves held a few dishes, cups and two glasses. On the countertop were neatly stacked piles of books. Debbie Macomber's *Cedar Cove Cookbook*, China Bayles' *Book of Days*, *The Cat Who...Cookbook* and *Brunetti's Cookbook* were next to the microwave. "Dorathea, what kind of life did you have?" Kara whispered under her breath.

She returned to the living room and sat on the couch, sinking into the soft leather cushions. Perez sat across from her in the chair and took a mini iPad out of his coat pocket. "This seems just like old times. You've come a long way, Kara. So, where do we start, Lieutenant Langley?"

Kara smiled at her old partner, "I'll look through the desk and you check out the titles. Maybe we'll be lucky and come across a clue that will lead us to why someone would want to kill this woman."

"Could it have been random?"

"No, she left this private library of hers and took a train to Kingston to sit on a bench in the dead of night. I'm sure she expected someone to be there to meet her. We just have to find out who and why."

The top drawer of the desk held writing supplies; some pencils, paper clips and note paper. The deeper drawers on each side were filled with notebooks, which Kara took out and placed on the desk. She opened one to discover pages of poems. She began to read and stopped only when she heard the sergeant's voice.

"She seems to be a lover of mysteries. This whole room is filled with them. Women authors on one side of the room, men on the other."

Kara collected mysteries herself and walked to the far wall to randomly read some of the authors out loud: "Margery Allingham, Sarah Cauldwell, Agatha Christie, Martha Grimes, P.D. James, Donna Leon, Ngaio Marsh, Louise Penny, Dorothy Sayers, Jacqueline Winspear."

She crossed to the other side and continued: "John Dixon Carr, Raymond Chandler, Arthur Conan Doyle, Dashiell Hammett, Tony Hillerman, Ellery Queen, Alexander McCall Smith, Rex Stout, Peter Tremayne, and on and on. What an amazing collection. I could just stay in this room and read forever!"

"Seems to me like that's what she did," commented Perez.

"Yes, I think you could be right about that. I'm going into the bedroom. Keep searching and call me if you find anything interesting."

Kara looked around and noted that the room was filled with children's books. She scanned the shelves and recognized many of them from her own childhood.

She sat on the edge of the bed. It was covered in an old-fashioned, cream colored, chenille spread. She ran her hand over the worn fabric. Attracted by a cover showing a tiny farm tucked in a hillside of autumn hues, she took the book from the bedside table and read the title, *A Berkshire Tale.* On an inside page was the picture of a kitten peeking out of quilted bag and an inscription:

> *My Dear Thea,*
>
> *You will always be welcome here with ZuZu, her Mama, her barnyard friends and our family on our farm in the Berkshire Hills.*
>
> *Your friend,*
>
> *Nick.*

It relieved Kara to know there was somewhere Thea Lorimar could have gone to be with people who cared about her. It caused her to wonder why this woman had chosen to lead such a lonesome existence in the middle of this crowded city.

In the office, Perez was continuing to walk around taking notes. "This room's full of history and travel and there's a section over there which seems to be all first editions of some really famous books. Maybe we should check them out?"

"Good idea, but I think I need to find out what the doorman can tell us. Could you go down and send him up?"

"Sure thing."

Kara moved around the office, touching the spines of the books' covers, trying to figure out who Dorathea Lorimar was. Was she a total recluse? Did she live her whole life inside the books surrounding her like the characters in a Jasper Fforde novel? Did she ever venture outside to mingle with the thousands of people who walked the sidewalks right under her window?

Sergeant Perez returned with Zimmerman. He sat in the chair and explained he'd been the doorman since October of 2007.

"How long has Miss Lorimar lived in this building, Dominic?"

"She's been here since I started the job. Someone told me she'd lived here all her life. Her parents had owned the apartment. I never met them. They died before I was hired."

"Is there someone in the building she was friendly with?"

"Not that I know. She may have spoken to people in the laundry room downstairs. There's a waiting area with a few chairs and shelves for sharing any books you don't want. I helped her bring some books down there one day. But she wasn't talkative. I doubt she made friends with anyone when she was doing her wash."

"What else can you tell me about her, Dominic?"

"As I said, she kept to herself. No visitors I can remember. She left the apartment sometimes and came back with groceries. I helped her bring the bags upstairs. There was never very much in them."

"Can you remember any conversations you may have had with her?"

"She wasn't a talker, like I said, but not because she was snobby. She just didn't say much. But she always smiled and she knew my name and she was considerate. When my first grandson, Arty, was born, I showed her his picture. She smiled and the next day there was a book and an envelope waiting for me when I came on duty. She wrote a nice note in the book and there was a twenty-dollar bill folded up and tucked into the envelope. I thanked her for the money and said it wasn't necessary and she told me to buy him something special because he was a special baby with a very special name. She always asked how he was doing. Called him Arthur. But that's the only time I ever had any kind of conversation with her. Oh, and another thing, she went out sometimes and returned with library books."

"Do you know which library she went to?"

"Probably the one at Bryant Park."

"You don't remember anyone coming to visit?"

"Sometimes in the bad weather, she had her groceries delivered from the Whole Foods Store down the street a ways. But no visitors. No friends. The night time doorman, Claude Pratt, begins his shift at three thirty. Maybe he can tell you something?"

"I'll check back with him to see if he noticed anything. Right now, we should head to the public library over at Bryant Park. I spent lots of time there during my days here in the city." Kara stood up and handed him her card as he prepared to leave. "Thanks, Dominic. If you think of anything else, please call me."

He nodded and shut the door behind him.

"So what do you think?"

"I think it's really strange she decided to leave this place last Sunday night and go all the way to Rhode Island only to be murdered when she arrived."

"I agree. We have a lot more work to do to find out who would want to kill this woman. Let's get to the library and see what we can turn up. We'll come back here later."

Kara went into the study to return the notebooks into the desk drawer, touching some of the books longingly as she passed by.

Kara had been to this building many times. She'd often spent evenings in Bryant Park, just behind the library. She headed straight for the main desk.

"Hello, Mrs. Flagstaff. Do you remember me?"

The tiny, silver-haired woman looked up over her spectacles and then took them off, placing them carefully on the counter.

"Well, young lady, of course I do. Kara Rodman. You look quite different out of uniform, dear. But I'd remember that intelligent face anywhere. You signed enough books out to start your own library."

"Thank you, Mrs. Flagstaff. I got married. My name is Langley now. I still read a lot. You'll be glad to know I belong to a book club in South Kingstown."

"Yes, I remember you telling me you were moving back to Kingston where you grew up and went to college. I've taken the train there on occasion. Lovely, charming, little station with its yellow clapboard and the olive green and black trim. I love the Victorian style of architecture. So much eye candy.

"Oh, and your libraries! Very small in comparison to this building, but I must say, both of the libraries I visited were magnificent. So much character!

"And there's the Daniel Chester French sculpture outside the one in Peace Dale. Such a talented artist. He did the Lincoln Memorial. He was a New Yorker, you know, although he created much of his work at his summer home in the Berkshires. A treasure trove of history to be found in those small New England towns."

She stopped to catch her breath and Kara jumped in.

"You remember my partner, Mrs. Flagstaff? We're here on official…"

"Of course I remember you," she informed the sergeant. "You came in with Kara sometimes. Congratulations, young man, I always knew you were perfect for each other!"

Kara blushed. She couldn't help but feel like a teenage girl when she spoke with the librarian. "Oh, no, Mrs. Flagstaff. This is Sergeant Perez. We worked together. We used to be partners. He's helping me on a case."

"Oh, my. Well, never mind!" The librarian took a few seconds to push back a strand of hair that had strayed from the tight little bun perched on the top of her head and then asked. "Have you moved back to New York?"

"No, actually I'm here investigating an incident that happened in Kingston."

"Did you come by train? Did I mention I love that little station?"

"Ah, yes." Before the librarian could start to reminisce once more, Kara quickly explained that they needed some information on a woman who lived here in the city. "She may have used this library. Her name is Dorathea Lorimar."

"Ah, Miss Lorimar, Thea. Yes, I know her. A very quiet woman. The perfect fit for a library. Bright woman, but very closed mouth, if you know what I mean. I always thought she knew more about books than I."

Kara felt this was quite a magnanimous statement from the librarian she'd come to know over the years.

"She certainly read enough. I haven't seen her in weeks. Let me check on that." She pulled up some files on her computer. "Yes, back in September, she returned some books, but didn't sign any out."

"Mrs. Flagstaff, I'm sorry to have to tell you this, but Thea Lorimar is dead."

The woman took a deep breath. "Yes, I sensed something was wrong when you asked after her. Lovely woman. I'm so sorry to hear the news."

"Did you ever have a conversation with her?"

"Not often, but one day, quite some time ago, she did request that I help her use a computer. I told her that one of our aides could assist her but she said she felt more comfortable with me."

"Do you remember what she wanted to use the computer for?"

"Let me think. I'm sure it wasn't anything to do with social media. She really wasn't the Facebook/Twitter type. It must have had something to do with research. Yes, she wanted to look something up on the Internet. I explained search engines to her. You know - Safari and Google and Yahoo and…"

"Mrs. Flagstaff, do you know what she was researching?"

"I need to ponder that for a minute. My memory is not the steel trap it used to be."

Kara suspected the woman's memory was still a steel trap.

"I think it had something to do with writing. Yes, I'm sure it did."

"What about writing?"

"Well, I don't know exactly. Once she grasped the concept of searching, she thanked me and I went on my way. I certainly didn't want to pry. And you know about curiosity and the cat. Do you still have your kittens, dear? George and Gracie, I believe you called them? I did love Burns and Allen. I miss the old comedy shows on the telly. So much gobbledygook now-a-days."

"George and Gracie are fine, Mrs. Flagstaff. Um, did Miss Lorimar ever speak with anyone else while she was in the library?"

"Oh, no, dear. Only me. Only me, poor thing. Her social communication skills were quite lacking from what I could determine. I always thought she would have made a wonderful mime. We had a speaker, I mean a performer, a mime, here to give a presentation just last week." She put the palms of her hands up and began acting out being stuck inside a box.

Kara determined this would be a good time to end the conversation, "Well, thank you so much for your help, Mrs. Flagstaff. I'm going to leave my card with you so you can call me if anything comes to mind."

The librarian mimed opening a door in the invisible box and put her hand out to take the card. "Stop by again, dear, when you're in the city and I'm very sorry to hear about Miss Lorimar. Lovely woman." Her hand brushed across her cheek as though taming another errant strand of silver as she left the box to return to her computer screen.

They went down the library steps to the police car. Glancing at each other, they both chuckled.

"She's a card! Where to next, Detective Langley?"

"We'll go back to the apartment. The person on night duty should have arrived for his shift by now. Hopefully, he can give us a lead."

A young man in uniform was waiting for them. He introduced himself as Claude Pratt and explained that Dominic had filled him in.

"Such a sweet lady, Miss Lorimar. But she seldom spoke with me. Just waved when she would leave for her night time walks."

"She walked around the city at night?"

"Yes. She would leave around nine or ten and come back a few hours later."

"Do you know where she went?"

"No, I think she just liked being out in the darkness."

"Why do you say that, Claude?"

"Once, when she returned, it had been snowing and she took off her hat, shook it out and brushed the flakes from her cape. She always wore that woolen cape in the cold weather. And she looked at me and said, 'What a marvelous time to be walking around the city!' It was December of last year and the holiday decorations were out. She seemed happy that night."

"And did she ever say anything else to you?"

"Not that I remember. Just 'Good night, Claude. Sweet dreams.' She said that each time she came back. Such a nice lady."

"Thank you, Claude." Kara gave him her card in case he had more information that might be of help."

When they'd left the apartment and were outside Penn Station, Sergeant Perez commented, "She seemed to have no enemies. No friends, either, but everyone we spoke with today said they liked her. Who would kill someone that sweet?"

"I honestly don't know, but I intend to do my best to find out," Kara said as she gathered up her things from the back seat to catch the next train to Rhode Island.

She'd eventually be returning to New York, but for now she felt she was getting nowhere learning about her murder victim. She wanted to talk with Darnell and his mother as soon as possible. She wondered why Lorimar was in South County eight years ago and if she had made any connections with other people in town.

Once settled on the train with a sandwich and a cup of tea, she opened the slim folder. Inside was one of the notebooks from the desk in the apartment. She'd taken it because she was interested in the verses within the pages and wanted to get to know more about this reclusive woman and what went on in her deepest thoughts. She intended to put it back when she returned at a later date. But for now, Kara sat reading the poems of one of the loneliest people she had never met.

Tuesday Night, November 17

They sat across from each other at the kitchen table. Arthur was not in a talkative mood and Neeka was trying her best to get him out of his funk. She'd made another of his favorites, Cheezy Chicken, in the slow cooker and he ladled the cheddar sauce over the noodles on his plate. He pushed around the broccoli spears imbedded in the cheese, but did not remove them. This was one of the recipes Neeka used to get some vegetables into him.

"Arthur, I had breakfast with JayZee today. You, know, the young woman in that feature article I'm doing about domestic abuse?"

"Humph."

She continued, "I told her I was moving in here with you and asked if she might want to join us for dinner some night."

"Humph."

"I thought you could invite Samuel and we could have meatloaf and mashed potatoes and peas. And I'd get you a lemon meringue pie for dessert."

He thought about this for a moment and muttered, "I like those pies you get from Gregg's. Are you going to get it from Gregg's?"

"Of course. And we'll pick up a cherry pie, too. Would you like to have a little dinner party next week?"

"Humph."

"Okay, then. It's a plan! Speaking of Sam, did you see him at all today?"

"I talked with him yesterday. He was cleaning out the gutters on his house. He's always working doing something. He's ten years older than me. I wish I had his energy. He mended that rock wall behind his property last week."

"So, what did you talk about?"

"Not much. He put a cap on the chimney at Fayerweather House. To keep out the raccoons this winter. 'Those critters can cause a lot of damage,' is what he told me. Said they used to eat raccoon meat when he was a kid."

"Maybe we should serve raccoon instead of meatloaf, then?"

"Humppphh!"

"Bad idea! Meat loaf it is! Did he have anything else to say?"

"Squirrels. He said squirrels can do their share of damage if they get inside a cellar or attic for the winter."

"Sounds like you had a sparkling conversation going there."

"Yup. And chipmunks. He calls them tiny rats with bushy tales. He's not crazy about chipmunks, either. They're all rodents, you know. Maybe you could do a story on the rodents of Kingston some day?"

"Maybe I will. I'm sure all the old Yankees will be buying up extra copies of the *Times* to send to their relatives who've moved far away. Like to Providence."

Providence was only thirty miles north on Interstate 95. She realized Arthur had totally missed the humor intended when he responded, "Mebbe."

Determining this conversation was leading nowhere, she took another tack. "So how did you keep yourself busy today?"

He thought for a moment and decided not to tell her about his visit to the doctor's with Ruth. "I've been reading that new book."

"Which new book?"

"The tart book."

"Tart? Do you mean Jacqueline Susann?"

They'd had an intriguing conversation about morals one evening when he found her reading *Valley of the Dolls*. In his words, "I am not a fan of that tart, Jacqueline Susann."

"Arthur, she hasn't written a new book. As a matter of fact, I'm pretty sure she's dead."

Arthur was staring at her like she had just sprouted horns. "What are you babbling about, Neeka? Who mentioned anything about that floozy?"

Now it was Neeka's turn to be baffled. "Arthur, you said you read the tart's book."

"So, what does that have to do with Jacqueline Susann? Why would I read a book by her? Besides, she's dead."

"Yes, Arthur. We've established that. Exactly what tart are you talking about?"

"The tart that wrote the book about the bird."

"Surely you don't mean Harper Lee, Arthur!"

"Not that bird! The other one. The little yellow one."

"Do you mean *The Goldfinch*?"

"Of course I do."

"All right, let's start again. So, you were reading Donna Tartt's book, *The Goldfinch*."

"Waste of time!"

"Why do you say that, Arthur? It got really good reviews here, although it was panned in the *London Sunday Times* and the *Paris Review*. I seem to remember *The New Yorker* wasn't too impressed with it either. But, Steven King liked it and it did receive the Pulitzer Prize last year. That's good for something? I think you'd agree? I may want to borrow it after you're done."

"You can have it now."

"You finished it already? That's amazing. It's a big book, Arthur, almost 800 pages."

"Nope, didn't finish it. Read half of it. Pure poppycock! Just what those snooty, pseudo-intellectuals would gush over."

"Maybe you should give it a chance and try to finish it?"

"Mebbe I'll give it a go again tomorrow, but I don't see much hope of changing my mind. I didn't like her last book either. Her first one was pretty good. Good lord! Thirty years to write three books. She needs better time-management skills if you ask me. She should have stopped after the first one."

"Like Harper Lee and *To Kill a Mockingbird*?"

"Yup, her other book, *Go Set Your Watch,* was a real dud!"

"We'll you've got a point there, Arthur. How long did it take for you to write *A Quiet Death*?"

"Less than a year. It took me less than a year. But I wasn't trying to impress anyone. Just wanted to write a simple book about what I knew. I had a really good life growing up. My father and mother were librarians. Now, my mother knew a good book when she read it. I didn't even have to go to school. Learned it all on my own surrounded by books and two great mentors. That's the only way to learn."

"It sounds perfect, Arthur, but we didn't all have the liberal parents you were blessed with."

"Oh, I realize how lucky I was. I do, Neeka. I miss them, you know. Especially my mother. She was wonderful. She took my stories and poems, typed them up and got them bound. Sent them off to that contest I ended up winning. I'd never have become famous if it weren't for her."

He stopped, put some pasta into his mouth and chewed for a long while before he was able to swallow it. Neeka knew what he was remembering and she leaned over to place her hand on his.

"Arthur, you can't blame yourself. It wasn't your fault."

He put his head down and brushed at his eyes. "She wouldn't have been there, if it wasn't for me. That taxi would never have hit her. She wouldn't have been in New York if I wasn't getting that award."

"She was so proud of you, Arthur. How could you have kept her away?"

"It was Karma, Neeka. A punishment. It should have been me. Not her. My punishment. Not hers. I'm tired. I'm going to bed. Goodnight, Neeka." And he pushed back from the table, rose from his chair and went to his room for the night.

"Good night, Arthur. Sleep tight," Neeka whispered as he shut the door behind him.

When Kara arrived home, she found Stewart in the kitchen making a pot of chamomile tea. Gingerbread and fresh whipped cream were out on the table. He took her coat to hang it up in the closet and she gave him a kiss. "You made gingerbread for me? How sweet!"

"I'd love to take credit, but Ruth dropped by my office this afternoon with it. She asked me to tell you she took Arthur for a check-up today. I told her where you were."

"I'll give her a call tomorrow. I've got something I want to show her." She went to her briefcase and took out the notebook. "These are some of Dorathea Lorimar's poems."

"What else did you pilfer?" Stewart asked as he placed a generous dollop of cream on a large slice of gingerbread and passed it to her.

"I would love to have brought home some of her books. You should have seen all the books." Kara had already told him about the apartment when she called to talk with him during the train ride home.

"The mystery section alone made me want to move in. But the place was utterly devoid of anything really personal."

"I think books are extremely personal. What you choose to read says reams about you," he remarked.

"What a wise and sensitive thing to say!" Patting his arm she added, "For a man, I mean." She pulled her hand away quickly before he could slap it.

"But honestly, there were no photos out, no art work, no decorations. Just wall-to-wall books and a couple of pieces of furniture. Although the couch was extremely cozy. And her closet! Stewart, she hardly had any clothes. And one pair of very sturdy brown shoes! What woman has only one pair of shoes?"

"Well, two pair to be exact," he corrected her. "The ones in her closet and the ones she was wearing when she died."

"Two pair of sensible, clunky, brown oxfords. It's just terribly sad. I went to her home to find out more about her and I discovered next to nothing. She was a quiet recluse who smiled and read books and went to the library on occasion and walked the streets of New York City alone late at night."

"And had a limited wardrobe and apparently wrote poems."

"There were other notebooks with stories in them. I only took the one."

"A New York recluse who wrote poems and stories," Stewart pondered.

"I was hoping Ruth could see something in the poems. She's good at analyzing things like that."

"Well then, the pilfering can be excused since it was for a good cause. So, what's your next step, Detective Langley?"

"I'm planning to get more details on the accident she had here eight years ago. Detective Sullivan spoke with Geralynn Sharkey, but I intend to interview her myself tomorrow. And I'd like to know where Dorathea stayed while in RI. I don't believe this was a random murder. There has to be a thread somewhere leading back to the motive. I'm not sure what it is, but I have a feeling it's hidden somewhere in her reason for having been here that summer. Why would a woman, with no apparent enemies or friends, for that matter, who is, for all appearances, a hermit, leave her apartment, get on a train and travel three hours to Kingston in the dead of night? It's too out of character. She had to have planned to meet with someone here. Someone who, for some reason, wanted her dead and I'm going to find out why."

Wednesday Morning, November 18

On her way to the newspaper office the next morning, Neeka stopped into the police station with a coffee for Leo.

"Here you go, large dark roasted, cream and three sugars."

"Thanks, Neeka. Here's the police report for you. You're early today."

"I've moved to Arthur's, so the station's right down the street and on my way to work. Your coffee will be delivered earlier now, on a regular basis."

"How's Arthur doing? He hasn't been here lately."

"Nope. I took his car keys and we've had long talks about the danger of driving with his condition. Although, sometimes he still refuses to admit he has a problem."

"He remembers being brought into the station all those times, doesn't he? He has to realize it's a big problem."

"He just says he gets tired and groggy and it causes him to mix things up. His memory is definitely not what it once was. Much of last night's dinner conversation was rambling and he kept going off on tangents."

"That's sad. Good thing he has you to look after him. So, you're moving in full time? Is that going to curb your style?"

"No way. As a matter of fact, how about meeting me when your shift ends? A new place called Mia's Kitchen in the Kingston Emporium. Food's great and there's a quiet spot with some comfy chairs by a little corner fireplace that's just right for sharing secrets among other things." She fluttered her eyelashes at him.

"I'm all for sharing. I'll ring you to make sure you're not off somewhere on a big story. Speaking of which, Lieutenant Langley went to New York City yesterday. She was checking the victim's apartment to see if there were leads as to why she was murdered."

"Did she find anything?"

"Not sure. She's in with Chief Lewis and her team now. If I find out anything, I'll tell you."

"Thanks, Leo. You're a good friend. What else is happening around here?"

"Nothing, really. Some cars broken into and a rowdy party down the line last night. College kids. Hey, how's your story coming along?"

"Good. It's almost done."

"We haven't seen Darnell in here for a while. I guess he's just about due with the holidays coming up. Thanksgiving's next week. I hate it around here on holidays. Putting families together drinking under one roof for a whole day is a menu for trouble. I've got night duty and the later it gets, the more calls we'll get."

"You're welcome to stop by, I'll be making a turkey and Arthur could probably use the company. It might keep him awake."

"I'll probably do that." Lowering his voice and leaning close to her, he said, "Speaking of Darnell, did you know about that accident he had a few years ago?"

"JayZee told me he'd had an accident, but I wasn't living here at the time."

"Well, come to find out, the person driving the car was Dorathea Lorimar."

"You're kidding!"

"Nope. That's how they found out where she lived in New York. She was in the system. She was brought in for questioning on the hit and run."

"Do they think there's a connection to the murder?" she asked.

Leo quickly stopped talking when the door opened and voices could be heard just inside. "The meeting must be over."

"Look, I'll see you later. We'll chat then."

"Thanks for the coffee, Neeka!" He batted his eyelashes at her as she turned to wave.

She laughed. "No problem. Bye for now."

The session had broken up with little accomplished. Kara made her report on what she'd found out in New York. Sergeant Shwinnard summarized what the team had been doing while she was away. He went over statements from people on the train or at the station that night. Shwinnard also had spoken with the lawyer who'd handled the Sharkey's case. No loose ends there, but the lawyer did tell him that Lorimar had been staying at The Rose and Thorn Bed and Breakfast on Kingstown Road.

Detective Sullivan had confirmed this by phone with Mrs. Alsop, the innkeeper. Kara planned to stop by there. So, at least there were some leads to follow, although they might not help with tracking down the murderer at all if she couldn't find a connection. But the fact that Dorathea had stayed here in the village proved she hadn't always been a recluse. Somehow, that was consoling to Kara who'd come to like this woman. She decided she would go up to Kingston and see what she could find out at the bed and breakfast and then circle around to Peace Dale to speak with Geralynn Sharkey.

The Rose and Thorn was one of a dwindling number of inns catering to summer tourists. With new hotels being built and seasonal rental houses down by the beaches, B&B's were becoming a thing of the past in South County. This one was close to the university. Visiting parents found it a convenient place for an overnight and of course it did well during Homecoming. But right now, just before Thanksgiving, there were only two cars in the parking lot.

Kara rang the bell and a short, curly-haired, older woman in a frilly blue and white apron answered. Her cheeks were a bright shade of pink and she reminded Kara of the Shirley Temple doll her mother had kept on a shelf in her bedroom.

"Good morning."

"Hello. Are you Mrs. Alsop?"

"Yes, I am. How can I help you?"

"I'm Lieutenant Langley from the South Kingstown Police. I'd like to ask you some questions about a woman who stayed with you."

"Certainly, Lieutenant. That nice young man, Detective Sullivan, called me yesterday."

"I know, he told me. I just need to go over some things."

"Of course. Come in." She led her through the hallway and into the kitchen. "Sit down, please." She indicated a chair at the head of the table. "I'm making another batch of cinnamon rolls. Would you like some?"

"Yes, I would. They smell delicious."

"Coffee or tea?"

"Coffee is fine. Just a little milk, please."

Mrs. Alsop was the model of efficiency. She brought a tray with cups and plates to the table, served the rolls, poured the coffee and sat down.

"What is it you'd like to know?"

"I'm looking to find out anything you can tell me about Dorathea Lorimar, the woman whose body was found this week. You told Detective Sullivan she stayed here with you in August of 2007. She had a car accident while she was here. A teenage boy was injured. Darnell Sharkey."

"Yes, I'm friends with Geralynn, his mother. Good woman. I do remember Thea and her accident. Actually, the damage was done to my son Tommy's car."

"Your son's car was the one involved in the hit and run?"

"Thea wanted to go to the rose garden at the University. She was planning on walking over. It's only a mile or so from here, but she'd turned her ankle and it was still sore, so my son lent her the keys to his car. She said she used to drive. Her beau had taught her. She thought it would be an adventure and Tommy figured it was just around the corner, so not much could happen."

"But how did she end up over on Ministerial Road? That's a few miles from here."

"Well, she'd read about the mountain laurel along the sides of the road and she wanted to see it for herself. After walking around the roses and hydrangeas, she decided to go out from the campus by the back way where Plains Road turns into Ministerial. Of course, there were no laurels in bloom. Too late in the summer for that. So, after riding all the way to Post Road, she turned around and came back. It was getting dark and she was in a hurry. That's when Darnell came off the section of bike path that crosses the road. He grazed the fender of the car and fell off his bike. He wasn't wearing a helmet. She heard the noise, she said later, but assumed it was a tree limb. Tommy noticed the damage to the car the next morning. Thea felt terrible and said she'd pay to have it fixed. When the mechanic got around to working on it, a few days later, he noticed some dried blood. He'd read about the hit and run in the paper. That's how the police ended up knocking on our door."

"Where was Thea when the police showed up?"

"She was still in her room. I called her downstairs and the police took her off to the station. She looked terrified. My husband went with her. He called Jim Ordman, our lawyer, who took care of things and brought her back here after she gave her statement."

"How was she when she returned?"

"I think she was in shock. Being taken to a police station, fingerprinted, the realization she'd hurt someone. All she kept saying was, 'I'm sorry, I'm so sorry'. I helped wash the ink from her fingers, made her a cup of tea and darkened the room.

"When I checked on her, she seemed to have retreated into her own world, sitting there in the chair in the dark. Later in the day, she told me she needed to take a walk. I asked if she wanted me to go with her, but she said she was just going down to the library.

"That night, Jim came to see how she was doing. He told her he didn't think the case would get to court. He'd spoken with the police and the boy's mother. It was obvious the teenager had run into the fender of the car with his bike. Thea told him to make sure all the medical bills were paid and to take care of anything else the boy needed. She wanted to talk to his mother to tell her that she would have stopped to help if she'd just known, but Jim said he'd take care of it. And he did. Geralynn confided to me that Thea had been very generous, even though she really didn't have to be.

"She stayed with us for two weeks. Hardly said a word. After everything was taken care of and papers signed, she took the train back to New York."

"Did you ever see or hear from her again?"

"She wrote us a thank you note. That was the last we'd heard from her. And then Detective Sullivan called yesterday. It's very sad. Who would kill such a lovely woman?" She poured more coffee for Kara.

"What else did she do while she was here? In the days before the accident, Mrs. Alsop?"

"Um, let's see. She walked around the village, visited Fayerweather House, the bookstore, the Artists' Guild and the library. She enjoyed reading outside on the bench under the oak."

"Do you know if she saw anyone? Did she have any visitors?"

"No visitors, but I'm sure she came in contact with people on her walks, although she never mentioned anyone to me."

"Could you give me the dates she was here?"

"I remember them well. August 8th to the 22nd. There were meteor showers - the Perseids. Thea said she didn't get to see many falling stars in the city. At least not the celestial kind."

"Thank you, for your hospitality and the information. Here's my card."

"I liked her and I'm sorry to hear how she died."

Kara's cell rang. It was Leo.

"More bad news, Lieutenant. Geralynn Sharkey was found dead in her kitchen a few minutes ago. Sergeant Shwinnard and Detective Sullivan are at the scene."

❧

She drove up the gravel driveway and parked on the side of the little cottage.

Sergeant Shwinnard came out to meet her. "Detective Sullivan is inside with the reporter from the *Times*."

"Reporter?" Kara was surprised.

"Yes, Annika Nordstrum. She's the one who found the body and called it in. Looks like it might be a heart attack, but I noticed some bruises on the arm, so we're playing it safe and treating it like a crime scene. Just in case."

Kara really hoped Geralynn had died of natural causes but the woman's connection to Dorathea seemed to be too much of a coincidence.

The porch door led directly into the living room where Detective Sullivan was taking Neeka's statement. Kara nodded and proceeded into the kitchen. Geralynn was lying on the floor on her side. It looked as though she had slipped from her chair, decided to stay where she was and take a nap. Her feet were tucked under the kitchen table. Kara surveyed the room and found nothing to signify a struggle had taken place.

An old copper teakettle sat on a the back burner of the stove. The toaster on the counter was plugged in. A slice of toast, partially eaten, was on a plate at the table along with a knife and an opened jar of blueberry jam, the bright red and white checked lid sitting beside it.

Kara bent over the body, noting the discolored bruising on her left forearm. She rose and stepped to the counter, touching the toaster and the teakettle, which was still warm. There was no dishwasher and the sink was empty. A wastebasket underneath held little. She shook it a bit. An empty muffin package, a crushed up cake mix box, a tea bag, some eggshells, a plastic container, balled up paper towels.

"Bag all this and get pictures. And don't let anyone else into this room except the medical examiner," she told the sergeant.

Taking one last look, she went past him into the living room. She glanced into the small bathroom and found towels neatly hanging on a rack. The shower stall held containers of liquid soap, shampoo and conditioner. The sink was clean. In the medicine chest were band-aids, opened pill containers, cough syrup, q-tips, a sealed container of

Norpace, nail polish remover, a tube of antiseptic ointment, a bottle of aspirin, roll-on deodorant, a toothbrush and toothpaste.

A small stairway led to two rooms on the second level. In one, the bed was made, the night table held a lamp and some magazines, neatly stacked, and the bureau was clear except for a lace cover, a small lamp and a mirror and brush set. She opened the door to the other room to find an unmade bed, clothes strewn on the floor and piled on top of a bureau. She wondered where Darnell was right now.

A voice called up to her, "Harry's here."

In the kitchen, she found the M.E. kneeling over the body and watched as he neatly and efficiently did his routine. He seemed to sense her presence behind him in the doorway. "You're keeping me busy lately. She's been dead only a short time."

"What about the bruising?"

"They're not fresh if that's what you mean. No other injuries I can see right now. Could have been a heart attack. Geralynn saw Dr. Gruber after that first one, three years ago. He put her on medication."

So, Harry knew Geralynn. She wondered if he was aware of the problems she had with her son.

"I don't like this, Harry. It doesn't feel right."

"Hmmm, well I'll have more for you later today." He tipped his hat and signaled for the emergency medical techs to come in for the body. Kara stopped them and instructed the sergeant to take a few more photos. Then, she took one last look at Geralynn Sharkey and told the EMT's they could place her in the van.

She sat down on the couch next to her friend. Neeka's face was pale. Kara took her hand, the sounds of the body being loaded onto a stretcher and carried out the kitchen door drifted into the room. Neeka dabbed her eyes. "I came to see if she was okay."

"Did you think she might not be?" Kara asked.

"Darnell's ex-girlfriend, JayZee met me for breakfast yesterday morning. I'm finishing up that story on domestic violence and wanted to do a follow-up with her before I published it."

"What did she tell you?"

"She said Darnell had been angry the last couple of weeks and he'd pushed his mother. I was concerned and decided to stop by to talk with Geralynn. I got busy yesterday. I've been moving some stuff to Arthur's place. I didn't get here until this morning."

"Did you phone first?"

"No, I just stopped by on my way to work. The front door was wide open. Nobody answered when I knocked."

"Darnell wasn't around?"

"No, but a white pick-up passed me when I turned into the road."

"Did you see who was inside?"

"A young black guy wearing a cap. I've never met Darnell, so I can't say for sure it was him."

"Was anyone else on the road?"

"No, just me. I parked in the driveway. The front door was open, like I said." Neeka took another Kleenex from her pocket. "I walked into the kitchen and," she took a deep breath, "Geralynn was lying on the floor. I checked her pulse and then I called the station on my cell." She swiped at her eyes again.

"Do you want me to give you a ride home? I can have an officer follow with your car."

"No, I'm fine. I think I'll stop by work and tell them what's happened. I have some things to finish up. Kara, do you think Darnell had anything to do with this? He'd found out about the article and was angry with his mother for talking to me."

"I hope not, Neeka. But I need to find him and talk with him. Do you know where I can find JayZee?"

"She should be at the nursing home around the corner. She has morning shifts so she can schedule her classes in the afternoon and evenings. She's been staying with friends. I was worried about her. I told her she could use my place if she wanted. She knows where the key is."

"Thanks. We'll talk later, Neeka. Take it easy."

❧

He couldn't stop thinking about what he'd heard. He knew what they were up to. Making it look like it was all his fault. His own mother. She was the worst. He suffered and she got the benefits and she just never let up. "Clean your room. Stop drinking. Get a job." He had a job. He hadn't told her, because he'd been keeping the money for himself. But he had a job!

She made him so mad. He punched the arm of the chair. Smashed his fist into it hard. They all made him so mad. It wasn't his fault. If they'd just let up on him, he could find some room to breathe. He needed to make a plan.

He bent down and rifled through his duffel bag. Finding what he was after, he got himself a beer from the fridge and popped some pills into his mouth. Stumbling into the bedroom, he threw himself on the bed and tried to figure out what to do next. But the room whirled around until eventually he fell into a fitful sleep.

❧

Wednesday Afternoon, November 18

The director on duty at Lakeside Nursing Center spoke with Kara and then went to find JayZee and bring her into the main office where they could have some privacy. JayZee knew something was wrong the minute she walked into the room.

"Detective Langley, is Darnell in trouble?"

"No, JayZee, sit down, please. I have something to tell you."

JayZee sat next to her on the couch.

"It's Geralynn, isn't it? Something's happened to her!"

"Yes, JayZee. Geralynn died this morning."

The girl looked as though she had been slapped. She said nothing.

"Neeka stopped by and found her in the kitchen. It appears she may have had a heart attack."

The girl sat stunned and after a time she began to shake her head slowly as she processed the news.

"Geralynn was like my mother. She took care of me. Better than my family ever did. She was so good to me. I should have never left the house. I should have stayed there with her." She began to cry. Kara took a Kleenex box from the desk and moved it next to her. When the sobs had somewhat subsided, Kara asked about the last time she had been at the Sharkey's house.

"I stopped over to see her on my way to work yesterday morning."

"Was Darnell there?"

"He came in while we were talking."

"How did he act?"

"He was riled up about something. He came in hollering, looking for a fight."

"Besides the yelling, was he violent in any way?"

"He came at me. Geralynn got in the way and he grabbed her."

"And then what happened?"

"I ran out the back door. She seemed to be having trouble breathing. She told him not to threaten me. He said he knew what the two of us were doing."

"What did he mean by that?"

"He'd heard us talking about the article Neeka was writing. He said he was going to find her and make sure she never published it. He threatened to kill us."

"JayZee, what kind of car does he drive?

"A 2008 Chevy pick-up. White"

"Do you know where I might find him?"

"I don't know. He hasn't been home much lately. He's probably sorry for what he did. He's always sorry after he does something like that."

"Where would he go? Does he have friends he could be with?"

"He doesn't really have any friends. Just some drinking buddies at the Road House in Richmond."

Kara got up to leave. "I'm really sorry, JayZee."

"She was so wonderful to me. I can't believe she won't be there when I stop by."

The girl began to cry again and Kara signaled for a nurse to come into the office. As she went through the door, JayZee suddenly asked, "Detective Langley, you don't think Darnell had anything to do with this? Do you?"

"I don't know, JayZee, I really don't know. If he gets in touch with you, call me right away. And whatever you do, don't go anywhere near him."

Darnell awoke and went to the living room. He sat on the couch, a gun on the end table by his side. He swigged some beer from one of the bottles at his feet, popped a few pills and then wiped his mouth with his sleeve. He wished he'd taken more clean shirts when he was at the house, but this one didn't smell too bad. He wanted to look nice for his girl. They'd been seeing each other since he'd broken up with JayZee.

Rusty had introduced them one day when she came by to skeet shoot. She was hot! Rusty called her Annie Oakley and she called him

Buffalo Bill. Rusty had a crush on her, but Darnell could tell from the beginning that she was really interested in him. She always let him do the talking. Not like other girls who went on and on about themselves. She was different. He could tell she was pretty keen on him. And why not? She called him "ruggedly handsome". Since he'd been taking the diet pills and lost all that weight, he probably could get any chick in the bar if he brought out his charm. He'd called the number she gave him, but just got voice mail. He didn't leave a message. She had the number at Rusty's house and said she'd ring. He could tell from the look she gave him when she said it that she would.

He took the gun and started loading it with ammunition from the drawer in the kitchen. He wished he could figure out how to open the rifle cabinets. They were beautiful. Rusty had taken him hunting before he left for Florida and it felt great to have a gun and point it at something alive, knowing in the next moment, it would be dead. He liked that feeling of power. No one would give him any shit if he showed up with a weapon like that. He'd like to see them try. He raised the gun in his hand and pointed it at the wide screen TV across the room. He'd like to see them try!

Vinnie brought her a cup of coffee and then sat at her desk waiting. "Neeka, you look beat. It's been a tough morning for you. Take the rest of the day off."

"I think I'll get some lunch and go home and work on my story. I'm not sure where I'm going with it right now with Geralynn gone and Darnell missing. But if Darnell had anything to do with her death, it puts a whole new twist on the story angle - 'Son Kills Mother in Uncontrolled Rage'".

"Do the police really think he had something to do with it?"

"I told them about the truck going down the road when I pulled into the drive. I don't know if it was his. I've never met him. I just know what JayZee said when she was telling me about all the abusive relationships she'd been in since she was a kid. It seems he's been getting worse since she broke up with him. He'd been giving Geralynn a hard time, so he could have caused her to have a heart attack. I got the feeling Kara was also thinking along those lines."

"Any new leads on the train station murder?"

"I'll find out at lunch. I think Kara feels there's a connection. According to Leo, they found out that Darnell was involved in a hit and run with the murdered woman."

"Now that is interesting. We should really be looking into it."

"I'm on it. I think I may have an idea where to find him. He has some buddies at the Road House."

"Well, let the police handle that. See what Leo has to tell you and then go home."

"I'm scheduled to be at the Town Hall Meeting tonight."

"Justin can cover that for you. He owes you."

"Thanks, Vinnie. I'll check in with you later to bring you up to date."

"Be careful, Neeka. Don't do anything foolish!"

Darnell didn't want to leave the house in case she called. But Rusty had an answering machine, so he thought he could take some time to go fire his new toy. He threw a few of the empty cans and bottles from the floor into a box, grabbed another beer from the fridge and headed outside.

After setting up the targets on the stone wall, he walked back twenty paces just like they did in those old cowboy reruns he and his mom watched when he was a kid. *Paladin, Have Gun Will Travel, Gunsmoke.* He turned and pointed at each target. Holding out his gun, he aimed, shot and missed. He moved in closer, firing again. One of the bottles shattered. "Take that, bitch!" He yelled out. *Now, that felt much better!*

He heard honking. Looking up, he saw Canada geese flying in a vee overhead. Pointing the weapon to the sky, he fired three times. The blasts resonated in the crisp afternoon air. The sound of the waterfall could be heard from the other side of the wall. Nothing fell at his feet. He was disappointed. "I need a bigger gun," he decided and went back into the house.

There was a message on the phone. Mizz Oakley would be stopping by later on and looked forward to seeing him. This day was finally getting better. He raised the gun above his head and pulled the trigger. Ceiling plaster rained down, startling him. He thought he'd fired the last round outside.

Brushing the plaster out of his hair, he took the gun to the kitchen and propped it against the wall. Checking the refrigerator for another beer and finding it empty, he opened the cellar door and looked down into the darkness. He found the light switch on the kitchen wall next to the door and switched it on. Propping the heavy door open with a brick, he grabbed the gun and staggered down the stairs in search of more beer and ammunition.

Darnell gazed longingly into the cabinets lining the walls. He dropped the gun and began banging on the glass fronts. Finally giving up, he took another six-pack with him upstairs to the living room.

He grabbed one of the beer cans, flopped on the couch and pulled the tab. Warm beer splattered over him. Reaching into his duffel bag, he placed some pills on his tongue and washed them down in one gulp. He picked up the phone, called Annie and left a message. "Bring food." Then, he rested his head on the back of the couch and fell asleep.

Wednesday Night, November 18

She rode down the long drive in the darkness. It was late, but a light was on in the house. She parked in the tall grass behind the hedges. Using the key ring flashlight to guide her steps, she walked across the pebbled drive and knocked on the front door. When no one answered, she let herself into the hall.

He lay there, smelling of stale beer, his mouth open, loud snores filling the room. She bent and looked into the open duffel bag. Removing the orange plastic pill containers, she examined the labels and placed one into her coat pocket, dropping the others on the floor. She moved into the darkened kitchen toward the light coming up from below and descended a narrow staircase into the cellar.

She entered the room lined with gun cases and spent some time trying to pry one of the locks open with no luck. A grating noise at the top of the stairs caused her to stop and listen. The door slammed shut and then the light went out. The cellar rooms had no windows to the outside and she was left shrouded in complete darkness. She heard footsteps and then another door closed overhead She called out, "Darnell!" and waited for him to come and set her free. She called out again. "Darnell! It's Annie!" No one answered.

Kara checked her emails. She was surprised to discover one from Mrs. Flagstaff. It said she might have some information which could be of help and to see her the next time she came to the city.

She hadn't intended to return that soon but when she arrived back at work, there were two phone messages. One was from Dominic. He'd found someone who'd known the Lorimars when Dorathea was a girl. Did she want to speak with him? The other call was from Sergeant Perez. They'd tracked down the Lorimar's lawyer. Plans were being made to meet him on Friday at the apartment. She immediately called and told Dominic she'd be in the city the next day.

She phoned Ruth, "Are you interested in taking a drive with me to New York tomorrow?"

"Sure, I have nothing on my calendar."

"We'll be staying overnight."

"A pajama party! Great!"

"I have an appointment on Friday with the lawyer and I'll need to talk to Mrs. Flagstaff. You could help me by looking over the books in the apartment."

"At your service, Detective Langley."

"I'd like to leave early, say around six.

"I'll be there."

❧

When Kara arrived home, Stewart met her at the door. "Hey, you're home early! I'll heat up some of the leftovers from last night."

"Sounds good."

"I'm surprised you could get away. How's the case going?"

"Geralynn Sharkey died this morning. I was going to see her after I interviewed the woman at the bed and breakfast where Dorathea stayed the summer she was here."

"What happened?"

"It appears she had a heart attack. We're not sure what brought it on. It seems suspicious to me that she'd die just when I'm investigating the murder of a woman she knew because of an accident her son was involved in eight years ago.."

"What about her son?"

"He's nowhere to be found."

"That does sound strange. So, what next?"

"I'm off to New York again tomorrow. I'm going to take my car. You'll have to survive without me for another night."

"If I didn't have classes, I'd go with you."

"That's okay. Ruth is free and we're going to have a Girls Night Out after I've done my investigating."

"Ah, it's Nancy Drew and Bess solving crimes in the Big Apple."

"You're showing your age. I was thinking more along the lines of Cagney and Lacey."

"Yeah, that sounds about right to me. Guess I'll just have to mosey on down to the old canteen and get together with my posse."

"If you're talking about the Faculty Center and that group of old codgers who show up for fish and chips every Thursday, I've got nothing to worry about, Cowboy. Knock yourself out! Now help me look for my boots and spurs. They're forecasting snow in the big city for tomorrow."

❧

Darnell had decided to go out and get something to eat. He was starving and Annie had never shown up. He went looking for her at the Road House, but the bartender said she hadn't been there since last week. He ordered a pulled-pork sandwich with fries and coleslaw. He smelled like beer. He was sick of beer.

The TV above the bar was set on a sports channel and he realized he'd been out of touch for the last few days. Everyone was getting ready for Thanksgiving football. He liked football. He'd been on his high school team for a few weeks until he got injured. He'd punched the player who'd sacked him and got kicked off the team for unsportsmanlike conduct. He smirked. *Yeah, like there's anything sportsmanlike about high school football played by a bunch of brainless, macho teen-age jocks!* He hated thinking back to high school. High school was hell on earth in his opinion.

Two women were sitting at the end of the bar. The redheaded one winked at him. He sent them drinks. They raised their glasses in a toast and signaled for him to come and join them. They made room between them and ordered him a whiskey. He began to think that this just might end up being his lucky night.

❧

She took out her penlight and shone it around the walls. "Hello? Can anyone hear me?" Her voice echoed. No one answered.

The light was dim, but at least she was no longer in the dark. She tried the door. It was solid and locked tight. There were no windows in the dirt cellar, no bulkhead leading outside.

Time passed with nothing but silence in the rooms above her. She roamed around, touching the damp walls, calling out louder this time, "Hello! Is anybody up there?" Still, no one answered. Her bag and cell phone were in the car. She felt lost without her phone.

Maybe when they realized she was gone, they'd track her to this hellhole in the woods of Richmond? Maybe by that time Darnell would return and hear her shouts? Hopefully, he'd be sober.

She went to the staircase and sat on the bottom step waiting for someone to find her. She propped her jacket on the stair above. She hadn't slept in almost twenty-four hours and she was exhausted. Resting her head on the coat, she eventually nodded off, sure that someone would come to rescue her.

Darnell was having the best time he'd had in ages. Women hanging all over him, buying him drinks. He didn't remember the last time that had happened. As a matter of fact, he didn't remember it ever happening.

Two guys with guitars began to play music. "Come on, cutie pie, let's get your booty movin'." The two giggling women pulled him from the barstool and guided him over to the middle of the room.

The short one, named Josie, grabbed him by his belt. "Sweetie, let's make ourselves a sandwich. You're the meat and Connie and me are the buns!" Darnell thought this was hysterical as they pressed their bodies against him and swiveled him around the dance floor.

At some point in the evening, they decided he was in no condition to drive, so they hoisted him into the back of their Jeep and took him home with them. Lying there, he looked up at the night sky as music from the radio came floating back, the two women singing at the top of their lungs. He decided this was the greatest damn night of his whole life.

Thursday Morning, November 19

Detective Sullivan sat across from Rick Carnavale in the interrogation room of the South Kingstown Safety Complex. The cab driver had been out late celebrating URI's win over Brown. His eyes were puffy and he wasn't smiling. He didn't seem to appreciate being called into the station this early.

"Thank you for coming in this morning Mr. Carnavale. We have a few more matters to clear up about last Sunday night."

Carnavale silently looked down at the baseball cap he'd just removed from his head. His thick black hair stuck out in all directions, causing Carl Sullivan to think of one of those round, spiky sea urchins he'd seen when he last took his five year-old son to the Mystic Aquarium. His son wanted to take it home as a pet. He bought the kid a plush penguin instead. Sullivan focused back to what he was doing by turning the pages of the file on the table in front of him.

"Mr. Carnavale, you told Detective Langley you picked up a fare from the Kingston Train Station at about 11:55 PM Sunday night and dropped your passenger off at the Grad Apartments up on 138." He looked over at Carnivale.

"Yeah."

"Where did you go after that, Mr. Carnavale?"

He sat thinking and Sullivan said, "There's a bit of a discrepancy about the time. You see, someone saw your cab pull into the Courthouse Center at 12:15. They were the last people to leave after the concert. It doesn't take twenty minutes to get from the station to the university and back. More like four minutes. Five minutes, tops."

After a brief hesitation Carnavale answered, "I went up a ways and turned onto South Road."

"I have here that you said you dropped off your fare and went back down 138 toward the station and stopped into the Washington County Center for the Arts."

"I did. Eventually."

"Eventually?"

"Yeah, but after I drove a ways down South Road, I decided to turn around. I went to the Arts Center to see if anybody was left over from the concert who needed a ride home. And to see my brother."

"So you went down South Road, but changed your mind and turned around?"

"Yeah."

"You left that part out when you were talking to Lieutenant Langley."

"It slipped my mind."

"How far did you go before you turned around?"

"I went a mile past the bike path, then turned in a friend's driveway and headed back."

"You didn't stop and go in to your friend's house?"

"No the front light wasn't on and the house was in darkness. If I'd seen a light on inside, I would've stopped to have a beer. I do that sometimes, but last Sunday I just turned around and headed back."

"Was anyone else on the road, Mr. Carnavale?"

"No cars. But there was someone on a bicycle coming off the bike path onto the road going real fast. I passed him on my way back."

"Could you give us a description of this person?"

"It was pretty dark. I caught him in my headlights. He was scrunched over the handlebars. Down low. Had on a dark shirt, gloves and a toque. He was going in the same direction, so I only caught him from behind for a second when I moved out to pass."

"Do you know what time this was, Mr. Carnavale?"

"It was after midnight. I don't know the exact time. I got back to the Arts Center around 12:15, I think. I didn't check my watch."

"And then you went in to help your brother clean up?"

"Yeah. I put some chairs away and we had a few beers. Sat outside on the steps and watched the meteor showers."

"What time did you get home?"

"I got in a little past one."

"Can anyone vouch for that, Mr. Carnavale?"

"My brother Gino could tell you when I left. I live alone. My wife died a few years ago after we first moved here."

"Where did you live prior to coming to South Kingstown?"

"New York City. My family's from Brooklyn."

Detective Sullivan had Carnavale's background information in the folder. He was asking questions he already knew the answers to and Carnavale realized this, so he was making it a point to be very cooperative.

"Where did you live in New York?"

"The Village. I had a small studio where I gave art lessons."

"You're an artist, Mr. Carnavale?"

"Yeah, painting and photography."

"Why did you leave New York?"

"My wife was sick. I brought her back here to be near her family. I stayed here after she died. It's a nice little town and I like being close to the ocean. I walk the beach a lot." Carnavale looked down at the cap still in his hands, "And I'm a big Sox fan."

Sullivan smiled at this. Not many New Yorkers would admit to being Red Sox fans.

"Mr. Carnavale, did you know Dorathea Lorimar?"

"No."

"Had you ever met her?"

"No."

"Is there anything else you may have forgotten to mention?"

Carnavale thought for a moment and then slowly shook his head, "Nothing I can think of."

"Well, thank you, Mr. Carnavale. That will be all for now. If you remember anything else about Sunday night, please get in touch with us."

Carnavale stood up and put the cap on his head. "I'll do that, Detective." And he left the room.

Detective Sullivan sat for a while adding to his notes and then dialed Kara's cell phone.

❧

Thursday Afternoon, November 19

Darnell slept in. He didn't get up until late afternoon. Groping around the dark bedroom, he found his clothes folded neatly on the bureau. He picked up the shirt and sniffed cautiously. Someone had done his laundry. The scent of lavender fabric softener clung to his socks. He brushed them against his face then dressed quickly. He could hear the sounds of a television set coming through the closed door and he went in search of someone who could tell him exactly where he was.

A redheaded woman with a bouffant hairdo sat watching a soap opera. He recognized the characters on the screen. His mother loved her soaps. He grew up sitting with her, a box of Kleenex between them as the actors in the *Bold and the Breathless* dealt with the daily drama plaguing their lives. The redhead turned when she heard the door open.

"Hello, Sleepyhead."

He flashed back on the previous evening. He recognized her but couldn't remember her name. It had been a long night. Everything was fuzzy. For some reason, this woman had aged a lot since then.

"Why don't you sit at the table, Sweetie, and I'll bring you a cup of coffee and something to eat?"

"Thanks," he mumbled.

"So, how do you like it?" she called from the kitchen.

"Like what?" He was almost afraid to ask.

"Your coffee. How do you want it?"

"A little milk and one sugar."

She came in with an oversized mug and placed it in front of him. It was just the right shade of brown and smelled even better than the coffee he loved from Dunkin' Donuts.

"You want some toast or a muffin? I've got a blueberry and a bran."

She touched the top of his head. Her nails were long and tapered and painted a bright orange to match her lipstick. He winced.

"I'll take the blueberry."

He looked around. The room was small. Cozy and neat. He got up from the table to bring his mug over to the couch and sat in front of the television, resting his coffee on a crocheted orange and blue coaster. His mother made them, too, and put them out on the coffee table when they had company.

She returned with his muffin. The canary yellow dish with a delicate green vine outlining the rim reminded him of the plates in his mother's cupboard. "Here you go. Do you want me to turn off the TV?"

"No, leave it on. I like soap operas."

He sat back as they watched a couple arguing on the screen. When his mug was empty, she took it out to the kitchen for a refill. He muttered to himself, "Finally a woman who knows how to treat a man. I could get used to this."

She woke up with a start, slumped at the bottom of the staircase. Light appeared to be coming through the crack under the door. She'd slept soundly although she remembered the last nightmare she'd had before wakening. People were looking down a deep well and she was at the bottom screaming at them to get her out. Someone yelled down, "You got yourself in there, now get yourself out!"

She listened for any sound that Darnell had returned. She took out her penlight and ventured into the room with the gun cases, moving the faint beam along the walls.

She flicked a switch on the wall. Nothing happened. A bulb on the ceiling in the far corner looked promising. It had a small chain dangling along the left side. She jumped up but couldn't reach it. Looking around, she found a rickety chair with no back. She placed it under the bulb and carefully climbed up to pull the chain. She blinked and almost lost her balance. The room was now filled with a faint yellow glow and she hopped off the chair to explore.

Gun cabinets surrounded her. In the outer room was a plastic laundry basket placed in front of an older model Maytag washer. She went to it and turned it on, quenching her thirst. Then she splashed her face and the cold sent a shock through her body. She turned off the water and continued exploring for a way out.

It didn't look very promising to her. She sat on the bottom step and tried to figure out what to do next.

New York was getting ready for the annual Macy's Thanksgiving Day Parade the following week. Trees were lit, decorations had already begun to appear and a light snow was falling as they left the hotel and walked to Bryant Park.

Mrs. Flagstaff was waiting for them at the front desk and after being introduced to Ruth, she took them over to a computer. "I kept thinking about what you asked me. You know? About what Dorathea was looking up on the Internet. I remembered she had checked some books out in September and I looked through them. They were all about copyrights and plagiarism. Look, here are the titles. I wrote them down for you on these index cards. I do love index cards, although they have become an outmoded method of note taking and filing and such. I loved the different colors, especially the bright neon pink, green and orange, and I'd..."

"Mrs. Flagstaff, thank you for all of this information on the books. Did you remember anything else about the day Thea was here?"

"Oh, yes, dear. The books jogged my memory. You see, when she left the library that day, she didn't close down her computer. I had to do that for her. You can't imagine how many people just get up and leave the computer without logging out or shutting down. The next person using it has to do it for them or I have to do it and it's…"

"Mrs. Flagstaff, what was Thea researching?"

"An author. I remember because she had looked up information on him a few years back. She had signed out his book at the time. *A Quiet Death*. I remember now, she returned it the next week and asked me if there was any way she could get more information on the author. I printed out some articles. There wasn't much. But I gave them to her."

"Do you remember when this all happened?"

"Oh, yes. It was back in the summer of 2007. I'd just returned with my husband from a cruise to Bermuda. It was lovely, but quite warm. Perhaps we shouldn't have gone to a warm climate in the summer, but it was our 40th Wedding Anniversary and he'd always wanted to take a cruise. We sailed on the …"

"Mrs. Flagstaff, I hate to interrupt, but this is important. Do you remember anything else?"

"I remember Dorathea asking me about train schedules and I got one for her. I didn't see her for quite some time after that. Months later, when she did come back to the library, she seemed different."

"How was she different, Mrs. Flagstaff?"

"Well, she was always a quiet woman, but after that she seemed timid and sad. Yes, I distinctly remember getting the feeling something bad had happened."

"Did she tell you anything about where she'd been?"

"I told her I'd missed seeing her and was happy she was back. And I inquired about her health, of course. But she never offered any information on where she'd been. She just said she appreciated my asking."

"Thank you, Mrs. Flagstaff. You've been a great help."

"It was no bother, dear. And how are George and Gracie? I just loved that show. Burns and Allen. You know, Gracie Allen was much smarter than she appeared. It was all an act."

"George and Gracie are fine. We have to go now, and thanks again for all of your help."

"Oh, you're quite welcome. And stop by the next time you're in the city. Nice to meet you, Ruth."

They left the building and walked toward Fifty-Sixth Street.

"Well, that certainly was interesting. Thea looked up information on Arthur before she came to South Kingstown in 2007. Do you think she may have returned there because of him? And could someone have followed her on the train?"

"I don't know, but things are finally beginning to connect."

"Oh and what's this about your cats? George and Gracie? I thought they'd crossed the rainbow bridge and gone to kitty heaven a few years back?"

"Yes they have, but not in Mrs. Flagstaff's world."

Dominic welcomed them when they arrived. He'd found a person who worked there in the 1960's. His name was Jonas Fulton. "I took the liberty of calling him and told him about Miss Lorimar. He remembers her and said he'd be glad to speak with you. Here's his number. He lives in Jersey now. Said to tell you to call any time."

"Thank you, Dominic. This will definitely help." He brought them up to the second floor and unlocked the door.

For the first few minutes, Ruth just walked around the apartment in awe.

"Kara, this place is amazing. She lived inside a mini-library."

"Yes, and apparently walled herself away from the outside world."

"I don't think I'd leave this place, either. Look, she has the entire Louise Penny series!"

"And in the other room, she has a whole section of valuable collections."

"So, where do we start?"

"Well, I have a few ideas. I'd like it if you looked through those first editions to see if you can find anything. An inscription or a notation. I'll go through these. And no reading. Just perusing, please, or we'll never get out of here."

"These first editions are in top condition. And she has quite a collection of Pulitzers. The ones I've looked at all appear to have been written before 1965. Oops!" A typewritten note slid out of the one she was holding. She picked it up and read it out loud.

> Please be advised that I bequeath all of my books to Mrs. Gloria Flagstaff, the librarian at the New York City Library in Bryant Park. Should she pre-decease me, these books should be given to the library in her name.
>
> Thank you.

It's signed Miss Dorathea Lorimar and dated November 30, 2007. Is that legally binding?"

"If that's her signature, then it most likely is. Either way, we really need to search all of these books carefully."

They continued on for an hour or so until Ruth found another note tucked inside a first edition, mint copy of Willa Cather's *My Antonia.*

> **My Dearest Thea,**
>
> **You have been so kind to our son and we know how much you cherish books. Please accept these as a token of our love and appreciation. Laura would have wanted you to have them.**
>
> **With much affection,**
>
> **Paul**

"Well, that explains where those books came from, but who are Laura and Paul?"

"Laura and Paul are the names of Arthur's parents. He lived in New York for a few years in the 1960's. That's when he finished writing *A Quiet Death.* He'd started it when he was a teenager, but completed it here in New York," Ruth explained.

"He never mentioned living in New York to me."

"He went back home to Iowa soon after his mother's accident. They'd come to a reception for him when he received the Pulitzer Prize, but his mother, Laura, was struck by a car and she died a few days later."

"I had no idea."

"He doesn't ever say anything about it. I know because he told me once when I asked him to speak to my class about his book. He said the book was a blessing and a curse and he'd rather not talk about it. But he did come to class once. He sat in the back and listened to the students discussing it."

"That's heart-breaking. No wonder he keeps to himself."

"Yes, he's comfortable in Kingston because no one ever bothers him about it. You know, he never wrote another book."

"He wouldn't ever have to write again. That book made him a fortune. It still is," Kara said.

"I always thought it strange, though. I mean, if you're a writer, then you have to write. You just don't stop because one book has made you rich and famous."

"Maybe his mother's death had something to do with that. Or maybe there are manuscripts hidden all around his house?"

"You mean like those poems Emily Dickinson's sister found hidden in the nooks and crannies of her house after she died?"

"Exactly! And now we have our connection. We just have to figure out why Thea came to Kingston last weekend. It must have something to do with Arthur. Who else would she be meeting?"

"Wait a minute. You're not actually thinking he killed her, are you?" Ruth looked at Kara, shaking her head no as if to elicit the answer she wanted to hear - that Kara did not believe Arthur capable of murder.

"Neeka says he's been acting rather strange lately. Not himself."

"We had a long talk at dinner the other night. What if he doesn't really have dementia? He could have something else that could explain his irritability and the tiredness and loss of memory. I took him to be tested for Lyme yesterday."

"But Neeka told me he'd been to a doctor. Right after the first time he was brought to the station."

"Did you see any reports? Or did you rely on what she was telling you?"

"I know you've never been a big fan of hers, but she really does care for Arthur. She's like a daughter to him."

"We'll see how the tests come out. He's been placed on antibiotics. If he notices a difference in the next few days, he just may have Lyme. It's rampant in Rhode Island."

"Have you found a copy of his book anywhere in this apartment?"

"Funny you should mention that. I haven't. But I'll keep looking. If they remained friends, she should have a copy, don't you think?"

They continued on their quest and as darkness set in and the lights were turned on, they hadn't found anything that would help. Ruth was in the bedroom checking through the children's books when she came across the one inscribed by Nick.

"Kara, did you ever get in touch with the person who wrote *A Berkshire Tale*?"

"I looked up his contact information and phoned. No one was home. I left a message. He hasn't gotten back to me. I'll try again. There doesn't seem to be anything else except her notebooks. I'll make another call if you look through them."

Kara dialed the number saved in her phone and a child answered. "Hello. Who's this?"

"This is Ms. Langley. Is your dad around?"

"Nope."

"Is your mom around?"

"Nope."

"Is anyone there with you?"

"Yup."

"Could you ask them to come to the phone?"

"Aunty Martha. Someone wants you to come to the phone," the child sang out.

This was followed by a click and a disconnect. A few seconds later, Kara's cell rang.

"Hello."

"Hello. I'm sorry, but your number is on our caller ID. Did you just call and speak with my niece?" an adult voice asked.

"Yes, I did. My name is Kara Langley and I wanted to talk to Nick Clauson."

"My brother isn't here right now. Could I help you?"

"I'm investigating the death of Dorathea Lorimar."

There was silence on the other end and then, "Thea's dead? When did this happen?"

"She died on Sunday. I called and left a message."

"I'm sorry. I've been babysitting and I'm afraid Lillian has been playing with the phone. She's been trying to dial her parents. They're on vacation. It's possible she's been erasing messages. Maybe I can help you?"

"We've been going through her things and we found a book written by Nick. The inscription led us to believe they knew each other."

"Yes, our father was good friends with her when he lived in New York back in the 60's. They dated for a while until he returned to the family farm when his dad became ill."

"Did Thea keep in contact?"

"Not really. But when Nick wrote his book, he went to New York and they met. That's probably when he gave her that copy. She never came to visit us, but Nick said she was a lovely woman. He'll be sad to hear she died. Dad often spoke of her and Arthur Jacobs and their time together in New York."

"Arthur Jacobs?"

"Yes, the one who wrote *A Quiet Death*. They were friends at about the time Jacobs became famous."

In the background, Kara could hear a young child crying. "I'll let you go. Could you have Nick call me when they return?" She thanked Martha and hung up.

Kara went to the office where Ruth was beginning to go through the notebooks. "I found something interesting. It appears that Arthur and Dorathea definitely were friends."

"That's strange. He never mentioned it on Monday or Tuesday when we were together."

"The newspaper doesn't come out until Wednesday. And the name of the victim was not released. He wouldn't have known about the murder unless Neeka said something to him."

"I'll phone him today and ask if he knows anything."

"Why don't you take care of that while I contact the number Dominic gave me?" Kara returned to the bedroom to place her call. She spoke with Jonas Fulton for fifteen minutes and then went to see how Ruth had fared.

"I wasn't able to get Arthur. No one answered. I left a message for him saying we needed to talk about Dorathea Lorimar." Ruth said.

"I'll tell you about my chat with Fulton on the way to dinner. It's getting late. Let's call it a day. We can finish this up tomorrow."

❧

Thursday Night, November 19

Lights had been strung along the streets, store windows were dressed up and trees were starting to twinkle everywhere. A soft snow had begun to fall as the two friends walked a few blocks to a restaurant Kara had frequented during her time in New York.

"Jonas Fulton was the doorman at that building for over fifty years. He remembers Thea as a little girl. He told me she was a very timid child and her parents were overprotective."

"Did he explain what he meant by that?" asked Ruth.

"He said that Dorathea stopped going to school at about the time she was twelve. Her mother was ill and she stayed home to care for her. Mr. Lorimar was an editor for a publishing company and he worked long hours every day."

"It sounds like a terribly lonely life for a young girl."

"From what Jonas said, she was a very bright child and her dad even brought home manuscripts for her to read and edit for him. She was quite good at it. Her father had bragged to him about his daughter on many occasions.

"Thea's mother died when she was fifteen and she didn't return to school. But one day, Mr. Lorimar came home with a young man, Walter Clauson, who was interning with his firm. He and Thea became friends and eventually were engaged to be married."

"That must have been Nick's father."

"It was. A few weeks before the wedding, he had to return to the family's farm in Massachusetts. His father had taken ill and he was needed back home. He wanted Thea to come with him, but she stayed in New York. Jonas said that he overheard them arguing in the elevator one evening. Mr. Lorimar refused to allow her to go."

"And so she ended up staying here, taking care of her father."

"Jonas thinks he died in the summer of 2007, but he's not sure of the date. He also told me there was another young man who was friendly with Thea. But he eventually stopped coming around, too."

"Do you suppose it was Arthur?"

"I think so because the timing is right."

They'd reached the restaurant and Kara looked through the window. "Ah, here's my old stomping ground. It's nice to see some things don't change."

They were seated within a few minutes and after settling in and ordering, they began to go over what they'd discovered about Dorathea Lorimar during the past few hours.

"In my conversation with Martha, Nick's sister, she told me her father had dated Thea. They were both friendly with Arthur when he lived here in the city. And he and Thea dated until his return to the family's farm in the Berkshires. They lost touch until his son, Nick, came to New York when his own book was published. Also, Arthur's father sent Thea their first edition collectibles after his wife, Laura, died. To thank her for her kindness to their son."

"I remember Arthur saying his parents were librarians, so that would explain their interest in first editions." Ruth added.

"But why not give them to Arthur?" Kara wondered.

"Well, Arthur doesn't have many books in his house. He reads a lot, but gets most of them from the library. Although, he loves to give books as gifts. It's obvious Thea treasured books, as can be seen from her apartment. They must have known this about her. Maybe they even visited her the first time they came to New York?"

"So we know there was some kind of relationship between Thea and Arthur fifty years ago."

"And Fulton's account would confirm all of this," Ruth added.

"And Mrs. Flagstaff told us Thea was looking up information on Arthur before she traveled to South Kingstown in 2007. That could have been just after her father died. We know she came to Kingston and stayed in the bed and breakfast across from Arthur's house that summer. They must have re-connected. Don't you think it would make sense? Why come all that way and not get together with an old friend?"

"But Mrs. Alsop said no one came to see her and that Thea returned to New York after the accident. Don't you think Arthur would have driven her around instead of her having to borrow a car from the Alsops?"

"I agree. That really makes no sense. I'll have to ask him about it when we talk. Hopefully, he'll remember."

"You know, the more I think about it, I really don't believe he has dementia. All of his symptoms are the same ones I had a few years ago when I was treated for Lyme. We'll find out soon enough when the blood test results come back," Ruth said.

"But what about the doctor Neeka took him to?"

"Doctors just don't seem to be up on this as much as they should be. There's lots of controversy surrounding diagnostic tests and antibiotic treatment. I can easily see an error being made. It happens every day."

"But to leap to a diagnosis of dementia. I don't know." Kara was still skeptical. "I really do hope his symptoms lead to some other explanation."

Their drinks arrived and they clinked their glasses in a toast to friendship.

"So," Ruth continued, "who would have motive and opportunity to murder Thea?"

"Well, she's leaving those books to Mrs. Flagstaff and the signed Pulitzers alone have to be worth thousands. She could have confided this to her. We still don't know what else is in her will."

"But we now know that Arthur and Thea were friendly with each other. That could be the connection to why she was at the train station last week. Maybe she was meeting him for some reason?" Ruth said.

"But that's not the only connection. Don't forget, she gave a pretty hefty out-of-court settlement to Geralynn after the accident. And, according to JayZee, Darnell is still holding a grudge because the money didn't go directly to him."

"Geralynn bought a house, which I'm sure will go to him now that she's dead. And all of his medical bills were paid. From the reports, it didn't appear he was hurt that badly. Just stunned and scraped up."

"But he blames all of his present problems on those injuries."

"Well, from talking with other police, he's always had a temper problem and was a regular at the station even back then."

"So, you think he's the most likely suspect for the murder?" Ruth asked.

"I don't know. Detective Sullivan called me this morning after he interviewed another person of interest. The background check was fine. The guy had lived in New York for a while. Sullivan found him rather likable. Typical man! I thought the guy wasn't very forthcoming when I originally spoke with him. A real 'Chatty Cathy'. I'll follow up on him myself when I return."

"Our connections with Thea right now are Mrs. Flagstaff, Mrs. Alsop, Arthur, Darnell and Geralynn and the doormen at her apartment. I just don't see Arthur and Geralynn as murderers. And do you really think Darnell would leave his own mother while she was having a heart attack?" Ruth asked.

"Maybe he didn't realize it was so serious? All I know is, he's a time bomb. And with the right motivation, from my experience, anyone can kill," Kara told her friend. "Anyone!"

❧

Friday Morning, November 20

Kara and Ruth sat across from each other enjoying a complimentary breakfast of homemade waffles topped with strawberries and whipped cream and drizzled with a dark maple syrup.

"We're meeting with the lawyer at noon, at the apartment, so there's plenty of time to continue searching and see if there's anything else that could help us," Kara said. "I'd like you to take a look at the notebooks and give me your impression of her writing."

"Do you know if she published anything?" Ruth asked.

"Nothing that I could find in with the other books."

"But she could have used a pen name."

"That's true. I jotted down authors I was not familiar with and thought you could look it over for me."

"Sure. I thought that notebook of poetry was quite impressive. I even wondered if she'd copied the poems from other poets, but I didn't recognize any of it."

"We can take them back home with us. I just have to sign for them. The lawyer will take care of all that this afternoon." Kara explained.

They checked out of the hotel, and drove the short distance to the apartment.

Dominic was there to meet them and brought them upstairs. Kara thanked him again for connecting her with Jonas. As he left, she told him to expect the lawyer, Mr. Matthews, around noon.

"I'll continue looking through the rest of the shelves of children's books in the bedroom. Make yourself comfortable and read. If you notice anything, just call out," Kara said to Ruth.

For the first half hour or so, Kara found nothing, but when she began to leaf through one of the books high up on the top shelf, papers came falling out. "Ruth, I think I've discovered more notes."

Ruth came in from the library and began helping to collect the papers gathered on the floor. They sat on the bed and began opening them.

"These all appear to be poems. Haiku poetry, actually." Ruth said.

They spread them out on the bed. Kara leaned over to read aloud the ones closest to her.

Bright lights, blinding lights
Illuminating dark streets
Inside lies blackness

Morning sunlight falls
Across my closely-tucked sheets
Holding me captive

The world awakens
Life goes on while here inside
My own quiet death

"Kara, let me see that last one." She read it again and said, "My own quiet death. Arthur's book, *A Quiet Death.* That's where he got his title. This can't be a coincidence. We have to get home and talk with him. He's the key to all of this," Ruth said.

❧

Friday Afternoon, November 20

There was a knock on the door and Dominic came in with the lawyer. Mr. Irving Matthews was much younger than Kara had expected. He appeared to be still in college or high school, for that matter.

"Thank you for coming here, Mr. Matthews."

"You're quite welcome, Ma'am."

Ma'am? Is he talking to me? She gave Ruth a quick glance, but her friend had turned away, suppressing a giggle.

"I would have been here sooner, but our office was notified only two days ago of Miss Lorimar's death."

"Yes, it took a while for them to track down who she had as a lawyer."

"Well, actually, Ma'am, we represented her father. Dorathea never contacted us after her father died and his will was read. She instructed us to write a document stating she would dispose of her belongings personally and that her wishes should be honored. She signed the papers that day and we've never heard from her since then except for the cashier checks she sent to us."

"What was the date, Mr. Matthews?"

"I have the document right here. It was signed on June 28, 2007."

"Is your father still with the firm?" Kara asked.

"No, Ma'am. He died in September, just a few months after that document was witnessed."

"Did he ever mention anything to you about the Lorimars?"

"He did make a comment once that Dorathea was a loyal and faithful daughter. I remember that because it's the same adjectives he used to describe our springer spaniel, Bertie."

Ruth and Kara exchanged a knowing look.

"Well, so far we've uncovered some of her wishes." She gave him the note about Dorathea bequeathing her books to the librarian.

"Her only other possession would be this apartment, I guess."

"Oh, no Ma'am. This didn't belong to her. When her father became ill, he couldn't work and so he was given a severance pay. After he died, there were debts. His illness had been quite costly, as was his wife's years before. The apartment was sold to pay them off and then rented back to her. Those books would be her only assets."

"Then how could she afford to live here?"

"I was able to obtain her bank statements and it looks like money was deposited regularly. Enough to pay for her rent and bills, but that's about it."

"Do you know where the payments came from?"

"As I told you, we were not retained by Miss Lorimar to take care of her finances. She gave us a written stipulation that she was going to leave instructions on where her assets would go after her death. Other than that, we've had no contact with her since then. The deposits were made into her savings on a quarterly basis. Here are the papers from the bank. I imagine the account will need to be closed. There isn't much left. Probably enough for a simple, quiet funeral, if she's cremated."

"Yes, a quiet funeral just like her life. It seems so sad."

Arthur never tired of roaming around the village reading the plaques on the historic 18th and 19th century buildings. He'd learned a lot about his neighborhood in the years since he'd visited to speak at the college's annual writers' conference and made the decision to stay. He often would go into the Kingston Free Library and sit for hours reading about the history that had taken place back in the days when the country was being formed. When people asked where he lived, Arthur would tell them "Little Rest."

Before 1826, Kingston was known as "Little Rest" because soldiers had rested here during the Great Swamp Fight of King Philip's War. At that time, the library was the Kings County Court House. He enjoyed the fact that he could sit in the actual spot where Rhode Islanders voted against ratifying the Constitution. They were wary of giving away states' rights to a stronger, federal government. Now, much of the village, including his house, had been put on the National Register of Historic Places.

Today he was feeling quite spry. He'd been on antibiotics for three days and it was making a difference. For breakfast he'd finished off the rest of his bucket of Kentucky Fried Chicken and then he set out. His first stop was across the street. Samuel was shoveling mulch around the rose bushes in the back garden.

"Hey, let me help you with that!" Arthur offered, throwing some compost on the ground near his friend. Sam was just finishing raking it around the red knockout roses when another shovelful landed on his boots.

"You do know that's alpaca poop you're throwing around?" he said as he shook some from his right foot.

"Sorry about that, Buddy. I guess I'm a lot stronger than I thought I was."

"You do seem a bit perkier today. What's that all about?"

"Ruth took me to her doctor. They tested me for a thing called Lyme and put me on antibiotics. Two drugs at the same time. Seems to be doing the trick."

"Well you look a lot better than the last time I saw you. You were mumbling, not making much sense and you dozed off once or twice."

"Yeah. It feels like I've been sleeping my life away lately. It's nice to finally be my old self again," Arthur told his friend.

He pondered this a bit as they worked together to finish the mulching. When they were done, he suggested going inside for a cup of hot coffee and a slice of homemade banana bread. They sat by the wood stove and Sam broke off a piece of an apple tree limb and threw it into the fire. "Ah that's a heady aroma. Brings back memories of when I was a kid."

"Memories are like strange ghosts," Arthur commented.

"What do you mean?"

"As you get older, they keep showing up to haunt you. Especially the bad ones. You think you've rid yourself of them and they come jumping back out at you. They're around every corner."

"Are you talking about your mother's death, Arthur?"

"Yes, that memory never goes away. No matter how many years have gone by, it's always in my thoughts. But there are others, too. Ghosts that need to be put to rest before we become spirits ourselves."

"And how can these ghosts be put to rest, Arthur?"

"The truth, Samuel. The truth. It's the only way."

"Amen to that, Brother!"

Arthur helped Sam carry the ladder over to Fayerweather House. He had some work to do up on the roof. He didn't go inside, saying, "I don't think they'd appreciate alpaca poop being traipsed all over the store."

"How about coming to my place some night next week? We'll celebrate!"

"Sounds great!"

"I'll get back to you with a time when I've checked with Neeka."

Sam patted his friend on the back. "You take care of yourself, Arthur. It's good to see you lookin' so well."

Arthur went inside the shop. It was quite festive and gave him a warm feeling remembering long-ago Christmases as a child. Everyone was happy to see him. A delightful aroma came from the little kitchen and they asked him to join them for lunch. All of them stood around the counter sipping mugs of hot chicken noodle soup. He hadn't felt this good in ages. He asked Cynthia to help him pick out a thank-you gift for Ruth. They chose a soft, tie-dyed silk scarf, emerald green to match her eyes.

After he left Fayerweather House, he decided to pay a visit to the Art Association. Walking into Helme House, he inhaled deeply. It smelled like wet clay and oil paints.

He thought about taking some classes now that he couldn't drive. He needed to find something to fill his time. Artists were setting up for a new display, but they stopped what they were doing and took the time to tell him about their work.

It all reminded him of a summer's day years ago when he looked up from his gardening and thought he saw an old friend coming from the inn next door to the studio.

Crossing the road, he'd followed the woman to the library and called out her name. "Thea?" She turned. It was her. The two had sat for hours on the bench under the oak tree. It had been a wonderful day.

Although it was cold outside, he decided to walk down to the library and sit on the bench for a while. He was happy to have these memories and he realized more than ever that good memories needed to be savored and cherished.

Kara answered her cell. It was Detective Sullivan calling with another update.

"They found Darnell's pick-up parked in the back of the Road House in Richmond. He wasn't inside. The bartender said Darnell had been there on Wednesday night."

"Does he have any idea where he might be now?"

"The bartender said he left with two women. They weren't regulars. But he did give us the name of someone who might have information. Rusty Russell. Lives in Hope Valley but spends time in Florida when it starts getting cold around here. Sergeant Shwinnard's checking on the address right now."

"What about the truck? I think you should leave it where it is and keep a watch on it in case he comes back."

"We're on it."

"Good. Keep me informed. I should be home in about an hour."

"Oh, and one more thing. We got a call from Lavinia Bloom at the *Times*. She's worried about Neeka Nordstrum. Says she hasn't been to work since Wednesday and no one's heard from her. She's concerned because she thinks Neeka may have gone to find Darnell for that story she's working on."

"OK, thanks. Tell everyone to be careful around this guy. He's dangerous. I'll see you in a bit. Inform the team we'll be meeting in my office as soon as I get back." She hung up and thought for a moment. "Ruth, try Arthur's house again. Ask if he's seen Neeka today."

She dialed the number. "It's his answering machine," Kara reached over and Ruth handed her the phone.

"Arthur, this is Kara Langley. We're trying to find Neeka. Can you call and tell us where she is? And I'd like to talk with you about an old friend of yours, Dorathea Lorimar. Please call Ruth or me when you get this message."

"What did you say about Neeka?"

"Her boss reported her missing. Said she's afraid Neeka went in search of Darnell for a story."

"Sounds like something that girl would do. Now I'm worried. Arthur's not at home either. I really hope she hasn't gotten him mixed up in all this."

Connie had made chicken salad sandwiches and homemade vegetable soup from the leftovers of last night's dinner. They ate lunch in front of the TV. Darnell was settling in comfortably, but he wanted to get his truck. As soon as their soaps were over, they were going to take the drive back to Richmond.

Josie stopped over to see if they'd made plans for the weekend. She had a pamphlet listing wineries in the area. There were a total of thirty of them on the Connecticut Wine Trail. That should be enough to keep them busy until Sunday and if they got the booklet stamped at each one they visited, they'd be eligible for a trip to some really great vineyards in Spain. None of them had ever been to Spain.

"This here is the farthest I've ever been from Peace Dale," Darnell informed them.

Connie and Josie thought this was hilarious and decided to celebrate the event by escorting Darnell to as many tastings on the Wine Trail as possible.

Kara met with the Chief and the team as soon as she returned from New York. She told them everything she'd learned in the past two days and they filled her in on what had been going on in South County while she was away.

It had been confirmed that Geralynn had died of a heart attack. Darnell still was nowhere to be found. Neeka Nordtrum had not been seen since Wednesday afternoon when she left work.

They were able to get an address for Rusty Russell and a Florida telephone number. Detective Sullivan had called and Russell told them he knew Darnell Sharkey. Sullivan had taped the conversation and replayed it for Kara:

"I hired him to watch my house while I'm away. Is something wrong?"

"No, Mr. Russell…"

"Call me Rusty. Everyone calls me Rusty."

"Rusty, we just need to talk with Darnell. We'll be sending someone to your house to see if he's there."

"Feel free to go inside, Detective. The doors are never locked. Could you call me back if there's a problem?"

"Sure Mr. Rus…Rusty. We'll do that."

Why she hadn't thought of it sooner caused Annie to swear under her breath. She checked the gun on the floor by the cabinets. It still had one shell left in it. She brought it to the bottom of the steps, aimed and fired. The door splintered and she bolted up the stairs. Putting her hand through the huge hole, she felt around the outside and unlocked the door. *Free at last!*

Friday Evening, November 20

The team arrived at Rusty Russell's house. No cars were in the driveway. The garage doors were open and nothing was inside except for a lawn tractor and garden tools. The sun had been out for much of the day and was beginning to set. There was a ominous quality to the storm clouds above the Usquepaug River as Kara and Sergeant Shwinnard moved toward the front door. Detective Sullivan took two officers around the back of the house. Kara knocked on the door and when no one answered, she called out, "This is Detective Lieutenant Langley from the South Kingstown Police Department." Again there was no response. Kara turned the door handle and it opened. Cautiously she and the sergeant stepped inside.

An empty beer bottle was on the coffee table and some cans and plastic pill containers were strewn underneath. A duffel bag was opened in front of the couch. Kara bent down to poke around inside. It held some crumpled clothes and more plastic pill containers with no information labels. A white coating of plaster covered the end table. Kara looked up at the gaping hole in the ceiling.

"I checked the bedrooms. Nothing's out of place. There's a beer can on the floor by the bed, blankets mussed up. Someone was here recently, but it seems to be empty now, Lieutenant, " the sergeant reported.

"Looks like someone was playing with guns inside the house," Detective Sullivan noted as he and the other officer came into the room from the kitchen.

"The back door was unlocked but someone took a gun to the cellar door. Blew a huge hole in the middle. Not only has the door been destroyed, but a large portion of the wall across from it needs some serious replastering."

Kara found the light switch and flipped it on. A dull yellow glow came up from the cellar. Kara moved cautiously with the sergeant close behind. A gun and empty beer cans were on the floor at the bottom of the stairs.

"Those need to be dusted for prints," she said.

"There's water pooled in front of this old Maytag," he said glancing around. Nothing much else."

Kara called from the other room. "Lots to see in here. Someone likes his toys," she commented as she checked the wall of glass-fronted cabinets.

"Some toys!" Sergeant Shwinnard whistled as he looked at the weapons around the room. They went back upstairs.

Through the living room window they could see two officers checking the garage. One of them came in to report, "We couldn't find anything in the woods. There's a cleared area near the river that's been used for target shooting. They're still looking, but nobody's around right now."

Kara shook her head. "Well, that's it. Darnell Sharkey's vanished, Neeka Nordstrum has disappeared and we still have a murder to solve." She looked out at the river wondering if it held any secrets. She hoped Neeka was somewhere safe. "Let's get a team in here to discover anything at all to help us find these people. I'll stop by Neeka's apartment and then I'll meet you back at the station when you're done here."

Ruth caught sight of Arthur coming out of the Kingston Hill Book Store. She went into the parking lot and waited for him to get into the car.

"Arthur, where have you been? I've been calling you every half hour."

"Ruth, how nice to see you. I bought you something." He took the box from his coat pocket and handed it to her.

She opened it up and looked at him with tears in her eyes. "Arthur, I'm so glad to see you. Oh, this is exquisite." She took the scarf from the box and draped it around her neck.

"I've been gone all day. Visiting with everyone in the village."

"I was so worried."

"I'm fine, Ruth. I was feeling much better and I wanted to thank you for bringing me to that doctor friend of yours. It felt good to be outside today, walking around. Oh, I've got to go back inside. I bought a book and left it on the counter." He hopped out of the car.

Ruth phoned Kara to tell her she'd found Arthur and he was safe and they were going to get something to eat. "I'll call you when we're leaving the restaurant." They agreed that Ruth wouldn't mention Lorimar's death to him until Kara was there.

When he got back into her car, Ruth said, "You must be starving. Where would you like to eat?"

"Well, everyone's been feeding me all day, but I could always fit in a meatball grinder. Could we go back to the Mews?"

"Sure. Do you want to stop at home first?"

"No, Neeka hasn't been around since Wednesday, so there's no one to worry about me. Except you."

"Arthur, did she tell you where she was going?"

"No. But she could be staying at her apartment. She's been real busy working on that special feature about domestic abuse. She was trying to get it finished for next week's edition."

"Kara said she stopped by and Neeka wasn't there. Would she possibly have gone home to her family?"

"She told me she was an only child, that her parents were dead. She always said I was her family. You don't think anything's wrong, do you?"

"Lavinia Bloom, her boss at the newspaper, called the police station concerned that Neeka had not been at work and they're following up on it."

"I hope everything's okay."

"I'm sure she's fine. Let's get you something to eat. I want to know all about what you've been doing and how you've been feeling this week. Have you received any information from the clinic on the results of your blood tests yet?"

"Nothing yet, but I'm feeling perkier."

"It would seem so. You've had quite a busy day. I'd guess from what you've told me, the antibiotics are working."

"All I know is, I'm looking forward to a meatball sandwich with cheese and peppers and a side of fries," he said.

"Your wish is my command," Ruth answered, touching the green silk scarf. "Remind me, did I tell you how glad I am to see you?"

"Yes, you did. You should get that memory of yours checked, Ruth. I know a good doctor I could refer you to."

Kara spent the rest of the evening at the station going over reports and compiling notes. It was dark outside, as she was getting ready to leave for the day a call came in to her cell phone, "Detective Langley, Darnell Sharkey just showed up in Richmond to get his truck. We're bringing him in," the officer informed her. She phoned Detective Sullivan and told him to finish up at Russell's place and get everyone back to the station.

Darnell was led through the back door of the station in handcuffs. The two women, who had driven him to the parking lot, were escorted in and placed in separate rooms for questioning. They all smelled of liquor and the redhead explained that they'd spent the afternoon visiting vineyards and doing wine tastings around Stonington. She pulled a booklet from her bag and handed it to the policewoman. It held the names of the vineyards and some of the pages had been stamped. An officer went to check on their story.

Kara assigned two officers to question each woman. She wanted to find out where Darnell had been for the last few days and did they know anything about Neeka Nordstrum.

When Kara entered the room, Darnell jumped up and started yelling at her.

"Why'd you drag me down here? I ain't done nothin'. I got my rights."

"Sit down, Mr. Sharkey. We have some questions we need to ask you."

She took a seat directly across from him as he continued to yell.

"I got rights. I want a lawyer."

"Sit down, Mr. Sharkey. I won't ask you again."

He could tell from the tone of her voice that it would be in his best interest to do what she said and lowered himself into the chair, glaring at her.

"You haven't been charged with anything yet, Darnell. If we decide to do that, you'll be allowed to call a lawyer or we'll get one for you. Right now we just have a few questions for you to answer."

He slouched down in the chair. "Questions about what?" he said insolently.

"Where were you late Sunday? Between eleven forty-five and midnight?"

"I was home with my mother. Ask her. She'll tell you."

"Do you know a Rusty Russell?"

"Yeah, I know Rusty. Why?"

"Have you ever been inside Mr. Russell's house?"

"Course I have. He invited me. I'm looking after it while he's gone."

"We've been to his house, Darnell. It looks like you're not doing a very good job taking care of the place. I don't think Mr. Russell is going to be happy when he gets home and finds the damage."

"Hell, it ain't my fault he leaves ammo in his guns. I was lookin' at it and it went off. Accidentally. I can fix that ceiling in no time. Just needs a little plaster."

"And what about the door?"

"What door?"

"The cellar door with the huge hole in the middle."

"I don't know nothin' about that. Someone musta broke in while I was gone."

"And where did you go?"

"I met those two women at the bar. They took me home with them. I been in Connecticut stayin' at Connie's for a couple of days."

"And was Annika with you, Darnell?"

"No, the other woman's name is Josie. Josie Fields. I don't know no Annika."

"You don't know Annika Nordstrum, Darnell? She's the reporter doing the story on JayZee for the paper."

"Oh, that bitch. The one who's been talkin' to JayZee."

"Yes, that one."

"I never met her but when I do, I got a lot to say to her. Getting my own mother to go against me. That's the lowest!"

"Your mother? Geralynn Sharkey?"

"Yes? What about her?"

"When was the last time you saw her, Darnell?"

"Monday morning. I haven't been stayin' at the house. We had a bit of a disagreement and I been watchin' Rusty's place."

"So you didn't see her at all on Wednesday?"

"No, I just told ya, I been at Rusty's."

"Darnell, your mother had a heart attack Wednesday morning."

He bolted out the seat, "Oh, my God. Where is she? I should go to her. You gotta let me outta here. She needs me."

"Darnell, she died. Wednesday morning, your mother died of a heart attack in her kitchen."

He looked at Kara in shock, slowly sat down and then raised his arms to the ceiling, letting out a pitiful wail. She stood looking at him hunched over the table sobbing, and left the room.

Neeka parked in the driveway and went in the back door of the house. Arthur was not in his downstairs' bedroom, so she checked the couch in the den. He wasn't there. She moved through the kitchen into the front living room and then came around again to check the bathroom.

"Arthur? It's Neeka, I'm home." she called. There was no answer.

He never went upstairs, but she decided to look there anyway. He was not in her bedroom nor the guest room and the attic storage room held only stacked boxes and extra furniture.

Downstairs again, she began to look for a note he may have left. She saw the light blinking on the phone in the kitchen and pressed the button. The first message was from Vinnie:

> "Arthur, I'm looking for Neeka. Could you call to tell me where she might be? She hasn't shown up for work today and I need to talk with her. Please tell her to call me right away when you see her."

The machine went on to the next few messages:

> "Arthur, it's Ruth. Call me when you get this."

> "Arthur, I called earlier and haven't heard from you. Please get in touch."

> "This is Ruth again. Kara and I are leaving New York and I should be at your place in a few hours. Call me if you get in. I'm really worried."

> "Arthur, this is Kara Langley. We're trying to find Neeka. Can you call and tell us where she is? And I'd like to talk with you about an old friend of yours, Dorathea Lorimar. Please call Ruth or me when you get this message."

There were two more callers leaving no message and another from a person Neeka did not recognize.

> "This is Wickford Junction Medical Center. You were in here on Tuesday with Ruth Eddleman for a check-up. Your blood tests have come back and we would like to discuss them with you as soon as possible. Please call at your earliest convenience. Thank you."

Neeka stood over the phone on the counter for a few minutes. Then, she made her decision.

Back at her apartment, she showered. Sitting on the bed, she realized how weary she was and she needed time to think. She had to find Darnell. Maybe he'd returned home now that Geralynn was gone. Yes, that was where she'd find him. She put her head on the pillow, closed her eyes and promptly fell asleep.

Kara went to speak with Connie who seemed very concerned about Darnell. She confirmed his whereabouts since Wednesday evening.

"Connie, what did you two talk about?"

"Just things. He liked soap operas. He used to watch them with his mama when he was a kid."

"Did he say anything about his mother?"

"He told me they'd been arguing a lot lately. Said it was his fault. He was feeling bad about a fight they'd had on Monday. Said he was going to apologize next time he saw her."

"Did he say anything else?"

"He loved my cooking. Oh, and he liked the lavender scented detergent I used on his clothes."

"Did he lose his temper at all when you were with him?"

"No. He was out of sorts a bit. I think he had a hangover. He complained of a headache and said he'd run out of his pills. I gave him a couple of Tylenol and he was fine."

"A headache? Did he tell you if he'd had headaches before?"

"He told me about that accident he had a while back. He wasn't wearing a helmet. Said he'd run into the back of a car when he was a kid. But he did admit the only time he really got headaches was when he'd been drinking too much or taking pills."

"Did he mention what kind of pills, Connie?"

"Yeah, he said a friend of his knew someone who worked in a pharmacy. She got him pills. He said he'd lost a lot of weight from some phen phen she gave him. I told him that stuff's nasty. Josie was on them last year and it almost ruined our friendship. I told her, "Josie, I'd rather have you fat and friendly than skinny and ornery."

"Did he give you this girl's name?"

"He called her Annie. Annie Oakley. Rusty introduced them. They used to skeet shoot out back near the river at his place."

"Is there anything else you can tell us about Darnell, Connie?"

"He was a lot of fun. What kinda trouble is Darnell in? Why is he here?"

"We needed to ask him about a few things. Connie, did you know his mother died?"

"No, Darnell never mentioned that. I'm sure he would have. He loved his mother."

"She died on Wednesday morning. I just told him the news. Connie, could you go in with him for a while? I think he needs a friend right now."

Kara brought the woman into the room. He was sobbing softly. She removed the handcuffs and Connie gave him a clean handkerchief. When he wiped his face, he looked at her. "This smells nice, Connie. Thanks for being so good to me." He lowered his head and his shoulders shook. His friend put her arm around him and let him cry.

Kara left them and stood outside observing through the two-way mirror. Detective Sullivan stood next to her.

"I spoke with Russell. Told him about the damage and that we had Darnell in custody. He won't press charges if Darnell does the repairs. He did say it could have been an accident. He says he sometime forgets and could have left ammo in the gun."

Listening to the conversation in the other room, Kara commented, "It appears to me that Darnell knew nothing of his mother's death. He said the last time he'd seen her was Monday morning."

"Do you think this is all an act?"

"No, I don't."

"So, where are we now?"

"We can't hold him for damages, because Russell is not going to press charges. He says he's had no contact with Neeka although he knows who she is. And she told me she'd never met him. It looks like he was not at the house when Geralynn had her heart attack and he says he was with his mother on Sunday night at the time Lorimar was killed, but now that Geralynn is dead, he has no alibi. We'll keep him overnight. I'm going to question him some more tomorrow. But it looks like our prime suspect may not be as guilty as we first thought he was."

❧

Friday Night, November 20

Arthur and Ruth stopped to pick up a lemon meringue pie on the way home. Ruth made tea for them. They were sitting at the table talking about the books Ruth would be using for next semester's class when Kara knocked on the front door. Ruth cut another piece of pie while Arthur went to let her in. She handed Ruth her backpack. "You left this in my car. How are things going with our wandering boy?"

"Our wandering boy has an bottomless pit for a stomach. He's been eating all night."

Arthur asked, "Have you heard from Neeka?"

"Nothing so far. Has this ever happened before, Arthur?"

"Well, most of the time she lived at her apartment, so I don't really know her habits. But lately, when she stayed here, she'd come in after work to cook dinner for us. Sometimes she went out to meetings or back to her place, but she never disappeared for three nights."

"Does she have a boyfriend?"

"She had lots of beaus and she mentioned someone who works at a pharmacy. I got the impression he was a lot younger than her. A student, I think? He was always giving her samples. Maybe she's gone off with him? You should check around here for an address book."

"That's a very quaint idea, Arthur. But today most people use their smart phone for keeping numbers. If she doesn't call soon, I'll look in her room to see if she's left a note or his business card."

Ruth jumped up from her seat, "We never looked at the phone. Arthur hasn't been here all day. There could be a message from her. She went to the phone, "That's funny."

"What is it, Ruth?"

"Kara and I called you at least five times today but there are no messages at all on your phone. Did you erase them?"

"No, I wasn't here most of the day."

Ruth and Kara went up to Neeka's room. It was neat and orderly. No photos adorned the walls, night table or bureau. Her drawers and closets were filled with designer clothes and shoes. Expensive leather luggage and a well-worn Burberry attaché case were stowed in the back of the closet. While Ruth looked in the pockets of clothes and in the luggage and briefcase, Kara searched the bathroom. Products were lined up on shelves above the toilet. In the medicine chest were three rows of amber-colored plastic pill containers. None were labeled.

"It would appear this girl collects drugs," she called out to Ruth. "How fortunate for her she has a boyfriend who works in a pharmacy."

"Kara, come look at this." Ruth was sitting on the bed with the briefcase opened next to her. She was holding an envelope and two letters. Kara joined her and read them both.

"What do you think we should do now?"

"I think we need to have a long talk with Arthur," Kara answered.

They returned to the kitchen.

"Arthur, we'd like to ask you about something. Let's go into the living room."

Ruth and Arthur sat next to each other on the couch with Kara in the chair facing them. She began the conversation.

"Arthur, did you ever know someone called Dorathea Lorimar?"

He looked at them and then answered. "Yes, I knew Thea. We met when I was in New York. She was engaged to a friend of mine."

"Have you been in touch with her lately?"

He hesitated before answering. "Is that why you were in New York? Is it about the book, Ruth? Did you go to see Thea about the book?"

Ruth and Kara glanced at each other and Kara nodded at Ruth who took his hand and said, "Arthur, Thea is dead."

They sat in silence and after a few moments he got up from the couch and went into his bedroom, closing the door after him."

"What next?" Ruth asked.

"It's been a long day. I need to go home and rest and I have a lot of things to piece together," Kara said.

"I'm going to stay here tonight. I don't want to leave him alone right now. I'll spend the time looking through Thea's notebooks." Ruth said.

"I'll be back to continue this conversation with him tomorrow morning. Call me when he gets up."

"I'll talk with you first thing in the morning. Give Stewart my love."

"Thanks, Ruth. You're a good friend. We're all lucky to have you around."

❧

Saturday Morning, November 21

Kara was up early and began putting her notes in order. Stewart offered to make her breakfast and keep her company.

"I was so sure Darnell was at the bottom of all of this and now, I just don't know. He has a motive, his truck was seen in the area that night and now that his mother is dead, he has no alibi. But he seems devastated by her death."

"Do you think he had anything to do with Neeka's disappearance?"

"That's what I have to talk to him about today. There are so many parts of this I don't understand. I've re-read his file and the kind of things he's been brought in for have been fights. When he's backed against a wall, he explodes."

Stewart poured her another cup of coffee. "How long has this been happening?"

"Since he was a teenager. He dropped out in the eleventh grade. Sergeant Shwinnard remembers him as a really overweight kid who was always being bullied. In his sophomore year, when he was 15, he assaulted a gym teacher. The report says the teacher was trying to encourage him to finish an obstacle course. Witnesses to the incident are on record as saying the teacher was taunting him. Calling him 'Fat Boy'. He finally hauled off and punched him. The teacher pressed charges and Darnell ended up being suspended."

"What about his girlfriend's account of his behavior? That domestic violence article Neeka is doing?"

"I spoke with JayZee. She said up until a few months ago, Darnell was never violent toward women. He got into fights when he drank sometimes, but never with women."

"So what would cause him to change?"

"Connie told me yesterday that a girlfriend of his named Annie, had gotten him some diet pills. Phen phen. He lost a lot of weight. But phen phen can really cause psychological problems with some people.

Mood swings, depression, even suicide. Add alcohol to that mix and it can be lethal."

"So he could have killed Thea?"

"Yes, it's possible. If he still blamed her for his problems, he has motive. I need to ask him some more questions before we actually charge him with murder. It's going to be a busy day."

The home phone rang and Stewart answered it. "Morning, Ruth. You're up early. Yup, she's right here." He handed the phone to Kara.

"Hey, did you get any sleep last night?" She listened as Ruth told her about what she'd found while reading Thea's notebooks.

"You really think so? Look, could you talk to Arthur this morning? Find out if your theory is correct? I'm going to the station to finish my interview with Darnell. I'll call when I'm done. Oh, and Ruth, don't let Arthur out of your sight."

She hung up and looked at her husband.

"Ruth just told me something and now I think I've figured out the motive."

❧

Ruth had spent most of the night reading the notebooks she'd placed in her backpack at Dorathea Lorimar's apartment. After she phoned Kara with her discovery, she went to the den and took Arthur's book down from the shelf. She was standing there when he walked into the room. "

"Ruth, what are these doing here?" He picked up one of the loose-leaf sheets from the coffee table.

"Do you know what they are Arthur?"

"They belong to Thea. They're her notebooks. Her poems, short stories, her book."

"Her book, Arthur?"

"Yes."

"*A Quiet Death* is her book?"

"Yes." He held out his hands and she gave him the novel.

"Do you want to tell me about it?"

"I'd like to talk about it. Now that she's dead, I think it's time." They sat surrounded by Thea's writings as Arthur told his story.

"I became friends with Walter Clauson when I first arrived in New York. I'm not sure how Thea met him. I think he came to drop a manuscript off to her father one day. They were friends, dated and eventually got engaged. He was so proud of her and talked about her all the time. One day he introduced us. I loved being with the two of them. They were protective and treated me like their little brother.

"She'd taken care of her mother at home for years. Mrs. Lorimar had Parkinsons. After her mother died, Thea was heartbroken and depressed. It wasn't until she met Walter that she even left the apartment. She finally had a life. Did you know, he even taught her how to drive? We had so much fun. And Mr. Lorimar was pleased when they became engaged. They planned to go down to the Justice of the Peace, at City Hall. I was going to be the best man. But Walter's father suddenly became ill and Walter had to go home to take care of the farm. He wanted Thea to come with him and I think she would have eventually. But then Mr. Lorimar had a stroke and she began her role as caretaker all over again." Arthur stopped and looked down at the book in his lap.

"Did she keep in touch with Walter?" Ruth asked.

"For a time they wrote, but then she stopped and at some point it ended."

"That must have been a very difficult time for Thea."

"It was. But she never complained. Not ever. Mr. Lorimar went back to work but he wasn't well. I finished the book I was writing. They'd given me a large advance. Mr. Lorimar and the others wanted changes made. I tried, but they weren't happy. No matter how much I edited, I couldn't please them. I was a failure and it was becoming obvious I'd be going home soon. That was when Thea took the book and made the changes for me. She was a marvelous writer.

"My novel was about my own mother caring for my grandmother. I remember them together so vividly. I wrote about it but I was really not good with novels. My strength was in poems or short stories. But Dorathea had an incredible talent. She could write anything. And it was magic, just like Walter had said. And she knew how to edit like a pro. It was Thea who gave my story life. She understood my mother. They'd both taken care of people they loved. They were kindred spirits and she infused a beauty into that book I never could have imagined doing." He held the book close to his chest and bowed his head over it.

Ruth waited and when she saw his hand move she asked him, "Arthur, why didn't you place both your names on it?"

"Oh, her father would have rejected that idea immediately. He was very old-fashioned. Her father never would have let her publish. He needed to keep her close at hand and wouldn't want fame to get in the way. You've read her manuscripts, Ruth. You can see the talent there."

"Yes, I did see it, Arthur."

He continued. "It was her idea to publish under my name. She said they were my ideas, I'd written the first draft. She insisted it should be mine and made me promise to say nothing of her role in rewriting it. She was afraid I would go back home and then she'd be left alone. She said it was best for both of us. And so it was published and it became a massive success. We never anticipated that.

"Thea was ecstatic. She was to be my date for the party the publishing firm was hosting for me. My parents were so excited and we looked forward to the celebration and then…." his voice faded.

"Arthur, are you still blaming yourself for the accident?"

"Ruth, it was my punishment. It was all a lie and someone had to pay."

"Arthur, you both agreed. You couldn't have known what would happen to your book."

"Her book, Ruth. Thea's book, not mine."

"And you returned home."

"Yes, I left Thea alone there with her father. I couldn't stand being in that city. I had to leave. I knew I didn't have the talent it would take to be a real writer. And I was angry with Dorathea, you know. I was so angry with her. If she hadn't talked me into the deceit, my mother wouldn't have died."

"You told me the other night you saw Thea again here in Kingston."

"Yes, you see, her father had died in June and after paying for the funeral, she had no money. I was the only one she could think of to turn to. She found out where I was and came here. It took her a few days to get up the courage to talk to me and I'm not sure she would have if I hadn't seen her across the street that day. Do you believe in fate, Ruth?"

"Yes, in some instances I do, Arthur."

"We spoke for hours. On that bench in front of the library. I was so glad to help her. I wanted to turn everything over to her. To give her full rights for the book. But she said that would be a big mistake. She lived a quiet life and could not see herself dealing with the notoriety that would come along. And she was fearful of a scandal. She didn't think people would understand and she didn't want me to be humiliated. We finally agreed I would send her money. She wanted just enough to pay her bills.

"The next day she had an accident and I helped her take care of the settlement. She thought she was going to be sent to jail. She was frightened and mortified she had placed me in such a position. She just wanted to go home. I took her to the train station and we sat on the bench by the bike path. We talked for hours. I begged her to stay here in Kingston but she needed to go home. I told her that when she decided to come back, I'd wait for her on our bench. She left, telling me she'd be in touch. I never heard from her again. I've been sending her checks regularly."

"And what about this year, Arthur? Did you know she was returning here on Sunday?"

"No. I didn't. When I became ill, when I started forgetting things, I worried that she wouldn't be taken care of if I couldn't send a check or I died. I wanted to arrange for money to be placed in a trust for her and I wanted to leave the book rights to her in my will. I sent her a letter, but she never wrote back to me. So, I planned on going to a lawyer about making the arrangements anyway. I wrote another letter telling her this."

"And you had no idea she was coming here?"

"No. What is it, Ruth? Tell, me please."

"Arthur, she took a train to Kingston last Sunday. It appears as though she was going to meet someone. It seems likely it was you she was coming to see."

"But I never heard back from her, Ruth."

"Arthur, someone met her at the train station. Someone knew she was coming here. She waited on that bench by the bike path. Late last Sunday night, Thea was murdered."

❧

It had been confirmed that the prints on the gun were Annika Nordstrum's. Kara had a lot of unanswered questions and she sent for Darnell.

When he was brought into the room, she noticed his eyes were still puffy and red from crying. He looked tired and weary and sat staring dejectedly at the wall. Kara watched from behind the window. She was weary, too. It had been a long week and she was ready to put this case to rest. Sergeant Shwinnard handed her two cups of coffee.

She entered the room and placed one in front of Darnell. He didn't move as she sat across the table and turned on the video recording device.

"Darnell. I'm going to ask you some of the same questions I asked yesterday and I'd like you to tell me the truth. You see, I think someone caused your mother's heart attack and I want you to help me find out who that was."

His gaze went from the wall to her face. "Someone killed my mother?"

"Someone caused her to have a heart attack. I believe that makes them responsible for her death."

"My mother was a beautiful person. Who would do that to her?" He looked around the room in a daze. "Who would do that?" he repeated louder.

"When was the last time you saw your mother, Darnell?"

"Monday morning."

"Not Wednesday?"

"No, Monday, I'm sure. I was hung over and still mad about Sunday. I'd come in angry and made a lot of noise."

"What time was this, Darnell?"

"Around eleven or eleven fifteen"

"Not after twelve?"

"I remember when I got in she was watching the news. It had just started. She always watches," he stopped and shook his head, "watched the news before she went to bed. Most times I'd sit with her. Lately I've been hanging out with some buddies and I get in after the news."

"Why were you early on Sunday?"

"I was supposed to meet a friend at the train station. She'd been in Boston for the day and asked if I'd pick her up and take her home."

"Did you bring her home?"

"She never got there. She called my cell and told me her train was late and she'd be on the next one and to wait for her at our spot. I'd been waiting in my truck, so I got out and went to sit on the bench by the bike path. To watch the stars. Lots of shooting stars."

"That was your spot?"

"Yeah, we used to go there after the bar closed. We'd talk. She liked to listen to me. I told her everything. She was a really good listener. I brought her a present. A cherry ring pop. She loves cherry. I left it there on the bench."

"Did she come in on the next train?"

"No, she called and said she'd decided to stay for another night and told me she'd see me later in the week. Said a friend would give her a ride."

"And so you left and went right home?"

"No, I stopped to get a drink and then I went home."

"Where did you stop?"

"At Fat Belly's in town."

"Did anyone see you?"

"Yeah. This guy was there. I knew him back when I was in high school. He was at a table with two other people. I didn't notice him at first, but he called out to me and when I turned, I recognized him. He was a gym teacher from the high school. He called me over…"

"What did you talk about?"

Darnell didn't answer.

"Darnell, this is really important. Would the people at the table remember you?"

"Oh, yeah, they'd remember."

"What did he say to you? When you got to the table."

"He said, 'Well if it isn't Fat Boy. Fat Boy here at Fat Belly's.'" Darnell hung his head.

"What did you do then?"

"It made me mad. They started laughing. I wanted to punch his face in again. But I didn't. I ran out of the bar and went home."

"And you had a fight with your mom?"

"I was kicking things around. Hollerin'. She told me to go to bed."

"What happened on Monday?"

"I woke up and heard voices downstairs. My old girlfriend, JayZee, was there. I overheard her talkin' to my mom about an article they'd been doin' with this reporter. It was on abusive relationships. I lost it. My mom told me to get out and not come back! That's the last time I saw her. It's the last thing she said to me. I feel so bad."

"Did you go to Rusty's after that?"

"Yeah, I waited for Annie to show up. I ended up drinking too much and shot up some bottles in the yard. And I put a hole in his ceiling. I'm real sorry about that. I'll fix it for him. He's been a good friend."

"Darnell, was anybody in the house with you?"

"No, I was alone all the time."

"What about the cellar door? Did you shoot a hole in that, too?"

"No, it was fine when I left the house. I remember moving the brick door stop and locking it up. I turned the lights out and went to the bar. To see if Annie was there. That's where I met Connie and Josie."

"You never went back to Rusty's?"

"No, Connie and Josie took me with them to Connecticut and I didn't get back here until the cops picked me up when I came to get my truck."

"You were with them since Wednesday night?"

"Yeah, I never went back to my mom's. I never told her I was sorry and now it's too late." He began to cry again. Kara took some tissue from her pocket and gave it to him. She left to speak with Sergeant Shwinnard.

"Get the information on that teacher and see if he can corroborate what happened Sunday night at Fat Belly's. Make sure you bring him in to do a formal witness statement and that all the times are included in it."

She went to her office and then returned to the examining room with a book which she'd brought from home that morning. She opened it to a marked page and placed in front of him. Pointing to a photo in the top left corner, she asked, "Darnell, do you know this person?"

He wiped his eyes and looked hard at the yearbook photo. "She's pretty. She looks like my girl friend. But she's a lot younger." He looked at it carefully. "Annie's prettier, though."

Shwinnard came in to tell her that Darnell's alibi had checked out. The gym teacher was coming in.

"Darnell. We're letting you go. We have some papers for you to sign and you need to stay where we can get hold of you."

"I'm going back to my mom's. I'll be there if you need to ask me any more questions."

Kara left the room with her college yearbook opened to Annika's picture and showed it to Detective Sullivan. "I was right. Send some officers over to search her apartment and put an APB out on her license plate. We need to find her fast."

❧

Neeka had awakened to the sound of her cell phone. The caller ID read "Kara Langley". She didn't answer it. Throwing some clothes in a shopping bag, she left her apartment. There were things she had to do.

She parked her car in a wooded lot nearby and walked to Geralynn's. She let herself in the back door with the key from under the mat. Taking off her coat and gloves, she sat in the kitchen waiting for Darnell, knowing he'd show up there at some point.

Neeka retrieved the pills from her bag, put on a mitt and took out two mugs from the cupboard. She crushed the pills into one of the mugs. She added water into both of them, popped in two tea bags and placed the mugs in the microwave. Each had a different tea bag and the Lipton's was his. She wrapped the pill container in a dishtowel, placed the sugar bowl on the table and put the mitt back on the hook.

❧

Saturday Afternoon, November 21

Hours later, the door opened. She heard him come into the house and go upstairs. Walking into the living room, she called from the front door.

"Darnell? Are you there?"

He ran to the top of the staircase.

"Annie. What are you doing here?"

"I heard about your mother, Darnell. I wanted to tell you how sorry I was."

"I'll be down in a minute. Just let me put on a clean shirt."

She went to the kitchen and turned on the microwave. He came into the room and gave her a hug. "I'm so glad to see you. I missed you this week."

"I went by Rusty's Wednesday night. You weren't there. And I tried to get your cell, but you weren't answering."

"It was in my truck. I met some friends and we partied."

"That must have been some party. I've been trying to get you for days."

He didn't want to tell her about Connie and Josie, so he said, "Yeah, them guys know how to have fun."

The microwave pinged. "I made us some tea. I thought you might want to talk about your mom with someone. Could you just get the cups from the microwave?"

He placed them on the table and stirred some sugar into his.

"Will you need help with making arrangements for her?"

"I don't really know what I should do. I've never had to make plans for anyone's funeral before." He took out the tea bag and sipped at his tea. It was too hot to drink.

"Well, what church did she attend?"

"Wakefield Baptist. I went with her when I was little. She sang in the choir." He began to cry and tried the tea once more.

"Do you have a family burial plot? Would she have wanted to be cremated?"

"I don't know. We never talked about stuff like that. I know I'll have to take care of things, but I don't know what to do."

"I'll help you. Don't worry. We'll figure this out together. Do you have any pictures of her? We could make a collage. Would you like that? You could write a message to her and tell her what you didn't have a chance to say."

Darnell went into the living room. With Neeka's help, he wrote a letter to his mother saying how sorry he was for what he'd done. Then he took out an album, which he placed on the coffee table. For a while they sat looking at photos, drinking tea and talking.

"I wish I'd been here that morning. I could have helped her. I didn't even know she'd died until the police told me."

Neeka stopped what she was doing and looked at him. "You spoke with the police? I thought you were with your friends?"

"I was. But the police found me. They took me down to the station. Told me my mom had died of a heart attack. They asked me questions. I think I'll just lie down for a minute. I'm really tired."

"Darnell, what did you tell them?"

"They asked so many questions." He put his feet up on the couch.

"Darnell, listen to me! What did you say to them?"

He closed his eyes. "It's nice you're here, Annie." His voice drifted off, then in a whisper she heard him say, "Thanks for being kind to me."

Annika washed out her cup, placing it back into the cupboard. Then she brought the dishtowel over, unwrapped the empty pill container and placed it next to the letter and the photo album on the coffee table. She looked down one last time at the sleeping man, went to the door and let herself out.

Ruth was in the kitchen when Kara arrived.

"I told him that Thea was murdered. We talked for a long time."

"How is he?"

"He's been in the den all morning, reading her notebooks."

"We released Darnell. He had a solid alibi. We're looking for Neeka. She's still missing, but I think I know where she's been since Wednesday. Ruth, I think she's the killer. I'm still piecing things together."

"I may be able to help with that. Sit down. I have a story to tell you."

After relating her conversation with Arthur, Ruth said, "I believe Annika may have been trying to stop Arthur from giving the rights of his book to Thea. She told everyone he thought about her like she was his family. She probably believed she'd be the one to inherit it."

"That certainly would be a motive. The book is worth millions."

Arthur came in to join them. He had the novel with him.

"Arthur, did Annika know about your friendship with Thea?"

"Yes, I wrote a letter to Thea, telling her about my illness. I asked Neeka to mail it for me. I remember she asked who Dorathea Lorimar was and I told her we'd been friends many years ago."

"And was that the letter Thea never answered?"

"Yes, so I wrote another letter last week."

"Arthur, is this the second letter you wrote?"

Dear Thea,

I've been quite ill lately and fear I may not be able to continue with our present financial agreement. I must talk to you in regard to the last conversation we had about the book. I intend to sign over the rights to A Quiet Death to you and need to meet with you to do the necessary paperwork.

Your friend,

Arthur

P.S. You can catch the last train from Penn Station. I'll have someone call you and arrange to meet you on our bench next Sunday night. Bring the manuscript. Please do this for me, as I'm becoming weaker every day and need to put my affairs in order as soon as possible.

He read it. "No, this isn't the one I typed. The envelope and the first part of the letter are the same, explaining I was ill and telling her about signing the book rights over to her. But the end is different. I'd never have asked her to come here at that time of night. Where did you find this?"

"It was upstairs in a briefcase in Neeka's room."

"Neeka had this in her room? But the envelope. The stamp's been registered, so it must have been sent. I don't understand."

"We assume this is the letter Thea received and it's what brought her here to Kingston on Sunday."

"She thought I would be meeting her?"

"Yes, Arthur. She expected to meet you. She brought the original manuscript with her. It was with this letter in the briefcase. And we also found newspaper clippings dating back to when you were in New York. Arthur, we have good reason to believe that Annika killed Thea."

"Why would she do that? She didn't even know Thea."

"She wanted you to leave the book rights to her. It was about the money, Arthur."

"But Neeka is like a daughter to me. I don't believe she'd do something so evil."

"Daughters sometimes can be quite cruel to their fathers, Arthur," Ruth said gently.

"She couldn't have done it. She was here Sunday night. Her car had a flat tire. I saw it. I found my keys and went out to the garage. Her car was blocking the garage doors. It was in the driveway all night. Sam changed the tire in the morning. I don't believe she could have done it! I have to think. To make some decisions. That book's been a curse from the beginning. I'm going out."

"Do you want us to go with you?"

"No, I'm not going far."

He placed the letter on the table and went to the hall to put on his jacket. They heard the front door close.

Kara and Ruth watched from the parlor window as Arthur walked across the road toward the Rose and Thorn. He stood at the bottom of the stairs. Mrs. Alsop opened the door. She spoke with him. He took her hand in his and shook his head, then turned toward Helme House.

He stood on the sidewalk looking in. Someone came to a window and waved. Justin rode by on his bicycle and stopped to talk to Arthur. When he left, Arthur continued walking until he was out of sight.

"Will he be all right?" Ruth asked.

"He needs time to process everything that's happened. It's not something we can do for him. He's lost a good friend and he's been betrayed by someone he loved and trusted. A daughter. He'll have to find a way to deal with it in his own time."

The phone rang in the kitchen and Ruth answered it. After a short conversation, she returned to the window where Kara was still keeping watch.

"That was my friend at the Medical Walk-In Clinic. She was calling again to speak with Arthur. He never answered her message and they're concerned. They want him to come back in as soon as possible to talk about his blood work. They've confirmed the Lyme but they also found other drugs in his system. Valium and Quaaludes"

"Drugs? Pills? Ruth, I have to go back to Geralynn's right now. And I need to talk with that taxi driver again. I just remembered something. Stay here and call me if Neeka shows up. Keep her here. And be careful."

"Do you think she'd come back, Kara?"

"She doesn't know what we've discovered. If she's the one who erased the messages, then she knows we were in New York and she's aware that Arthur went to the doctor this week. Neeka's convinced she's clever. Smarter than all of us. I believe she'll show up somewhere, as soon as she figures out a plausible story to keep Darnell as our prime suspect."

Arthur sat on the wooden bench encircling the old oak tree on the front lawn of the library. He was remembering that day eight years ago when his good friend had returned to him. It was one of the nicest days he'd ever spent since moving from New York. There weren't many happy days after that. But he'd learned to love this little town and had made some new friends. That was something, at least.

He thought about the day he and Neeka had sat talking and getting to know each other. He just couldn't believe she'd hurt him. She was his family. Family would never be that cruel. A daughter would never cause that kind of pain.

Arthur stared over at the church. The windows of Fellowship Hall were lit up. People were gathering. He wanted to be part of this happiness right now. The church bell began to toll as he crossed the street and walked up the path. A banner outside the hall announced, *"Whoever you are and wherever you are in life's journey, you are welcome here."*

A woman greeted him and brought him to a table where others were talking and laughing. They welcomed him and he sat down. A young child came over to him with some bread and a bowl of soup. He looked around. Tables were set up with people decorating wreaths with greenery and candles. He remembered them from his childhood – Advent Wreaths. The candles symbolized hope, love, joy and peace. The child asked if he'd like to make one with her after he'd eaten. He told her he would.

"Thank you for coming in, Mr. Carnavale. I won't keep you very long. I was reading the statement you gave to Detective Sullivan. You're an artist? A photographer?"

"Yes."

"You have an exhibit at the Fine Arts Building on campus."

"Yes. I teach a few classes there."

"Photographers are very observant, I would think?"

"We're used to focusing on our subjects, so yes, in a way."

"Mr. Carnavale, I need to clarify one more thing."

"And what would that be, Detective Langley?"

"You stated that you saw a person on a bicycle the night of the murder."

"Yeah, he was coming from the bike path."

"Do you remember anything about the bicycle, Mr. Carnavale?"

"It was too dark to see a color." He thought for a minute. "Just your regular guy's bike."

"It was a man's bike?"

"Yeah, the bar sloped across not down, but…" he stopped. Kara waited.

"Come to think of it, I did notice something funny."

"What was that, Mr. Carnavale?"

"As I passed by, I thought I saw streamers."

"Streamers?"

"Yeah, those things they put on kids' handlebars. Shiny strips like Christmas tree tinsel, you know? They glinted in my headlights."

"Thanks, Mr. Carnavale. I appreciate your stopping in again."

"You're welcome Detective. Nice doing business with you." He shook her hand and went out, closing the door behind him, leaving her alone in the room as she made one more phone call before returning to Arthur's.

"Justin, I'd like to stop by and take a look at your bike. Thanks."

Saturday Night, November 21

Quietly Arthur let himself into the house and went upstairs to Neeka's room. He sat on the bed next to the brief case. He recognized the initials. Thea's father's case. The one he carried to work every day. He took the manuscript in his hands and held it for the first time in years. So many memories came rushing back, overwhelming him with powerful emotions.

He began to look through the clippings. The announcement of his Pulitzer; Annika's review of his book from the *Connecticut Current*; his mother's obituary; articles about him coming to RI to speak at the summer consortium.

"Arthur?"

At first he thought he was dreaming, but he heard the voice again, coming from the hallway.

"Arthur?" A figure came into the doorway and stood there looking at him. "Do you remember when we met? We talked for hours?"

He didn't answer.

"I was so pleased you wanted me to be your friend."

"Friendship is a gift, Neeka. It should be cherished."

"I cherish our friendship, Arthur."

He looked directly into her eyes, "Neeka, I just learned an old friend has died. I'll never see her again to tell her how much she means to me. Someone took that away from me. Someone murdered her." He waited for her to say something, to explain away what he now knew to be true.

"Oh, Arthur, I'm sorry. You must be feeling so alone right now. But you have me and I won't leave you. You're my family, Arthur."

He stood up, sadly shaking his head and left the room to go downstairs, away from her. She let him by, following behind. When he got to the top of the landing, she moved furtively toward him, her arms outstretched. A voice from the door of the guest bedroom caused her to jump back.

"Hello, Annika. We've been waiting for you."

Ruth placed herself between the two of them and stood staring at the startled woman while Arthur walked slowly down the stairs. At that moment, the front door opened and Kara appeared. Ruth came down stairs with Neeka following.

"Neeka, we've been looking for you for days, " Kara exclaimed. "I'm glad you're here. I've got a few questions I need answered, not the least of which is your whereabouts since I saw you on Wednesday at Geralynn's."

Ruth sat down at the kitchen table next to Arthur and put her hand on his. Annika stood near the stove looking down on them.

"Unfortunately, I was indisposed. I went to the office and after talking with Vinnie I decided to go looking for Darnell, to get his side of the story."

"Weren't you afraid he might hurt you? You said you saw his truck leaving Geralynn's. He must have been in quite a state."

"No, I didn't think I'd be in danger."

"But you were the reporter writing the story he thought was about him and JayZee."

"I got a friend to introduce me to him when I first started researching the article. He just knew me as Annie. He didn't know I was a reporter. I wanted to see Geralynn's abuse by her husband from her son's viewpoint. We became quite close, but he was very volatile at times and I didn't realize how obsessed with me he'd become. That day, I knew he'd be at Rusty's. When I went to see him, we fought and he forced me into a cellar and locked the door."

"You mentioned a Rusty. Who was he?"

"He was the guy who introduced me to Darnell at a bar where they hung out."

"And where was Rusty while you were locked in his cellar?"

"In Florida. He let Darnell stay at his place while he was away."

"So, did Darnell eventually let you out?'

"No, he left me there and never came back. He probably thought I wouldn't get found. That I'd die. I waited and then finally I took a gun and blew my way out."

"Do you have any idea where he is now?"

"No, but there's one thing I have to tell you. Darnell confided in me that he killed a woman. Her name was Dorathea Lorimar and she ruined his life."

"That woman was my friend, Neeka," Arthur said softly.

"I know, Arthur, and it's partly my fault what happened to her. And I'm so sorry she died. That's what we fought about. Darnell knew she was meeting me to get money for the manuscript. The original one she said she wrote. He was waiting for her and he killed her."

"Darnell killed Dorathea Lorimar?"

"Yes, he saw me as his girlfriend and he'd do anything for me. When I told him about her blackmailing Arthur because of the book, and how angry I was, he told me he could take care of it. She agreed to sell the manuscript to me. I wanted to protect Arthur. I told Darnell all this and he was furious, but I never imagined he would kill her."

"Do you think he had anything to do with his mother's death?"

"He's been really out-of control and abusive lately and I saw his truck leaving when I pulled into her drive on Wednesday."

"Your statement said you were stopping by with her pills?"

"Yes, JayZee used to take care of that, but I did it for her since she broke up with Darnell. We figured it would be better if she stayed away from the house. He threatened to kill her."

"I noticed when I checked the medicine chest there was the container you'd just delivered and some other pills, too. But there were no labels on the containers. Do you know anything about them?" Kara asked.

Those must be Darnell's diet pills. He wanted to lose some weight, so I gave him some of my pills."

"Where do you think Darnell is now?"

"I told you, he took off from Rusty's Wednesday night after locking me up and I haven't seen him since."

"Then you'll be relieved to know I was with him earlier. He's in the hospital."

There was a knock on the door and Ruth got up to answer it. Sergeant Shwinnard and Detective Sullivan came into the room. Sullivan nodded to Kara as the sergeant announced, "Annika Nordstrum, I'm arresting you for the murder of Dorathea Lorimar and for the attempted murder of Darnell Sharkey."

She looked up at him in stunned silence, then started toward the back hallway. He moved to her side. She turned and pleaded, "Do something, Arthur. This isn't right. I'm being framed."

Shwinnard read her her rights, placing the handcuffs on her. As he led her out to the police car, once again she implored her friend, "Please, Arthur, tell them I'd never do anything to hurt you."

Arthur sat shaking his head in stunned disbelief, not saying a word.

Kara stayed with Arthur so that Ruth could go home for a change of clothes. She called Stewart to tell him that the case was closed and she would be home later. He said he'd have tea waiting and told her he'd really missed her this past week.

"I love you, Kara."

"I love you more."

She ended the conversation quickly before he could tell her he loved her even more than more. Once they started this conversation, it could go on forever, although she had once insisted that loving someone "the mosty, most" was the highest level there was. Nothing was more than mosty most she contended.

Ruth returned and Kara told her she'd see her at Sunday Service.

Arthur heard the front door close and looked up. "Are you staying tonight?"

"Of course. I'll be here for you, Arthur."

"I'd like to go to church with you tomorrow morning, Ruth."

"Yes, if you'd like."

"I want to talk to your pastor afterwards to see if she would do a memorial service. When we sat on the bench at the library that day, Thea looked over and said she thought it looked like a fine church."

"It is, Arthur. They're very caring people. I know Thea would want you to do this for her."

"I'm going to bed. I'll see you in the morning, Ruth."

"Good night, Arthur."

He went to his room and closed the door.

Sunday Morning, November 22

The morning was bright and clear as Arthur and Ruth walked down the red-bricked path to the Kingston Congregational Church. The bell in the tower rang out thirty-three chimes.

Members were at the door greeting those entering the church. Stewart and Kara were waiting inside. He recognized people from the village sitting in the pews talking quietly to each other. His new young friend who helped him with the Advent Wreath waved to him as he walked past. Her family smiled at him and he smiled in return. Cynthia and Betty were sitting with Samuel who stood to take his friend's hand when Arthur moved into the pew in front of them.

A deacon began the announcements, "Whoever you are and wherever you are in life's journey, you are welcome here."

Arthur was not sure how much longer his life's journey would be, but he still had some unfinished things he needed to take care of. He listened to the organ and thought back to that summer's day when he and Neeka had sat on the stone wall out front talking for hours. He wasn't sure he could bear the sadness he was carrying inside. Ruth reached over and touched his hand and he knew in his heart there were people he could depend on. People he could trust. Cherished friends.

After the service, Ruth and Arthur spent time with the minister. Stewart and Kara went out for breakfast at Mia's and then he brought her to her office and left to do the week's food shopping at Belmont's.

"Call me when you're done and I'll come to get you. There's a Livingston Taylor concert tonight at the Courthouse Center and I bought us tickets. Love you."

"Love you more."

Sunday Afternoon, November 22

Kara walked into the front door of the station and Leo buzzed her inside.

"How are you doing?" Kara asked.

"I'm okay. Still trying to get my head around all that's happened in the past week. I thought she was my friend. I'd never have guessed she could be that devious."

"She had us all fooled, Leo. Every one of us. Except maybe Ruth."

After looking through her notes and checking messages, Kara called an officer and asked that Ms. Nordstrum be brought into the interrogation room.

Annika sat, head down, with her hands folded on the table. She didn't look up when Kara came into the room.

"Neeka, I have some questions that need to be answered. You can have a lawyer present if you'd like."

"I don't need a lawyer. I've done absolutely nothing wrong," she informed her friend through clenched teeth.

Kara sat down across from her and turned on the video recorder.

"Sunday, November twenty-second, two thousand fifteen, 2:10 PM. Detective Kara Langley and Ms. Annika Nordstrum present in the interrogation room."

Annika sat up straight on hearing her name. Her fingers brushed back the strands of hair whisping at a face now rigid with barely suppressed anger.

"Annika. Can you tell me the details surrounding the death of Dorathea Lorimar?"

"I wouldn't know about that since I wasn't there."

"We have evidence that conflicts with your statement. Evidence we found at your apartment and in your room at Arthur Jacob's."

"Then it was probably planted there."

"Who would have placed a briefcase belonging to Thea Lorimar's father in your closet?"

"It was given to me by her real killer."

"Her real killer?"

"Darnell Sharkey."

"Why would he do that, Neeka?"

"He was crazy about me. I told him Thea was blackmailing Arthur into leaving the rights to his book to her and how hurtful it was to me and he decided to fix it."

"Why do you think she was blackmailing Arthur?"

"Why else would he write that letter about sending her money? Why would she even have his manuscript?"

"Did you read that letter?"

"Arthur gave it to me to mail it for him. He told me all about it."

"We found two letters inside the briefcase in your room at Arthur's. One, written by him to Dorathea Lorimar, had never been mailed. The other, he says, had been changed."

"Arthur hasn't been himself lately. He doesn't remember anything very clearly."

"He's feeling much better now. You know that Ruth took him to her doctor. He's been diagnosed with Lyme Disease."

"He has dementia!"

"No, it's Lyme. He also had other drugs in his system causing him to display signs of dementia. Do you know anything about that?"

"How would I know if he was over-medicating himself?"

"I spoke with your friend."

"Which friend would that be?"

"The young man who's interning at the pharmacy. He gave me an account of the samples he's been giving you. Valium, Quaaludes, PhenPhen. He even said you asked him to get you a knock-out drug."

"Why would I ask for a knock-out drug? It's not like I'd ever need a drug to lure someone into coming home with me. I have more than my share of boyfriends."

"Justin Kelly is another one of your friends, I believe."

"He's a reporter. I work with him and we go out sometimes."

"I spoke with Lavinia Bloom. She told me Monday was your day off but Justin, who should have been working that morning, called in sick. That's why she sent you to cover the story."

"She called me in the morning. The woman was killed late Sunday night. I was out partying with friends and was home well before she was murdered. Besides, I had no way to get to the train station. On my way home, I'd noticed something wrong with my car when I parked it in the drive. The left front tire was almost flat. Ask Samuel. He lives across the street from Arthur. I called him and asked if he'd fix it for me. He said it was late and he'd come over the next morning. And it was blocking the garage, so I couldn't have used Arthur's car. I was at home when that woman was murdered. Arthur was there."

"You said you were partying earlier that evening?"

"A few of us met at The Mews. You have their names. They'll vouch for me."

"Was Justin Kelly with you?"

"If you question him, he'll tell you I gave him a ride home."

"He takes his bicycle to work every day. He rode it to the Mews on Sunday night. It has colored streamers on the handlebars. I've already spoken with him. He said his girlfriend put them on as a joke."

"So, what has that got to do with anything?"

"He said his bike was in your car that evening."

"And I left it at his place when I dropped him off."

"No. Actually, you used it later that night to get to the train station. It isn't very far from Arthur's, if you take the bike path from the South Road entrance."

"Justin's a bit mixed up. He was really drunk. I stayed with him for quite a while after I took him back to his apartment. And I left his bike in the hall downstairs."

"He mentioned he'd been sick. Hung over. But he said he hadn't had that much to drink because he knew he had work the next morning. I told him he should get himself checked out at the medical center."

"He drank plenty and he was really out of it when I dropped him off."

"Well, he did take my advice and there were traces of Rohypnol in his system. The knock-out drug you asked your friend to get for you. We didn't find it in the collection of drugs you had in your medicine chest. We did find diet pills and some pills we had tested that turned out to be just placebos."

"None of that proves anything."

"We'll be entering it in evidence. You see, I think you drugged Justin to use his bicycle and to make sure he wouldn't be at work the next day. That way you'd be sent to cover the story."

"That's ridiculous! You should be interrogating Darnell Sharkey, not me!"

"We have been questioning him. And we've done a search of his house. We found more evidence there. You see, Darnell took the wrong pills from the cabinet when he went to Rusty's. He thought he had the phen phen but, instead, he had a container with some of his mother's heart pills in his jacket pocket."

"Well, no wonder she died. If he was walking around with her pills."

"Strangely enough, the real pills were mixed in with placebos. The same ones we found in your apartment. You were bringing her a new prescription that morning. You've been delivering her prescriptions for a few months now and mixing in placebos so her dosage would be off."

"She was already dead when I got there! I told you that!"

"Then why did you take time to place the unopened prescription in her medicine chest? I checked everything when I came by the morning you found her in her kitchen. The container had your prints on it."

"At this point, Neeka stood up and pounded her fists on the table. I thought you were my friend, Kara. Why are you acting like I did these awful things?"

Kara turned off the recording device. "Because, Neeka, you did these awful things. I'm advising you to get a really good lawyer, Neeka. You underestimate people because you think you're smarter than all of us. And you use people. But you can't control everything, Neeka. You made assumptions and that was your mistake. You trusted that all of us would never see through the pretty outer shell into the real you. We almost didn't."

She waited for a response.

Annika pointed her finger accusingly at Kara. "I'm being framed. I want a lawyer, now! And make sure it's a man!"

She turned the recorder back on, "Detective Kara Langley - interview with Annika Nordstrum ended at 2:40 PM."

❧

Darnell was still very weak. Kara had phoned Connie and she'd come to the hospital to be with him. In the afternoon, he was released. She helped him to dress and brought him back to Geralynn's. There they made plans.

JayZee stopped by and stayed for the afternoon. He asked if she would help choose a dress for his mother to wear and the three of them brought it to the funeral parlor. There would be a memorial service in the Baptist Church where she once sang in the choir.

That night Connie drove Darnell to the cemetery and they stood at the graves of his grandparents where his mother would be laid to her final rest. Overhead a lone star fell from the sky.

Monday Afternoon, November 23

Late Monday afternoon, after spending the morning with her team, Kara was ready to give her report to Chief Lewis. She entered his office confident they had enough to convict Annika Nordstrum for the murder of Dorathea Lorimar.

She placed the folder of statements and evidence and the videotapes on his desk. She wanted to go over the information they'd gathered and answer any questions the Chief might have before the press conference scheduled for later in the day. Captain Joaquin sat across from her taking notes as she went through the events of the past week.

"On Sunday, November 15, 2015, Dorathea Lorimar took the train from Penn Station in New York City and arrived at Kingston Station at 11:45 PM. She waited on a bench at the far end of the adjacent parking lot for Annika Nordstrum to pick her up and bring her to the home of Arthur Jacobs. Lorimar and Jacobs had met through a mutual friend, Walter Clauson, in New York City during the 1960's when Jacobs was writing his book, *A Quiet Death*. Lorimar's father had been an editor at the publishing company handling Jacob's book."

"Kara, why so late? And why was Nordstrum there to meet her?"

"In the past few years, Lorimar had become more and more reclusive, only venturing out at night. Ironically, she felt safe in the darkness. Jacobs wrote a letter telling her he feared he was losing his memory and he wanted to make sure she would continue to receive the financial help he'd been providing her, should something render him unable to send the monthly checks. He'd entrusted the letter to Annika Nordstrum to mail. Nordstrum read the letter and assumed Lorimar had been blackmailing him. So, she took matters into her own hands and laid out a plan to put an end to the blackmail permanently. And to get back the original manuscript of Arthur's book, *A Quiet Death*, that she knew was in Lorimar's keeping."

"When was this letter sent?"

"The first letter was never mailed. In July, Arthur was stopped for erratic driving. He submitted to a Breathalyzer and it proved he hadn't been drinking, so he was released. He'd been having difficulties for a few weeks. It was recently found that he'd developed Lyme Disease causing him to be easily fatigued. It was also around this time that Annika began putting tranquilizers in his food."

"Why would Nordstrum do this to him?"

"Greed and control. She'd been helping Arthur with his bills that summer after his memory troubles began and saw his bank statements. She realized how much money the book and film were bringing in and she also became aware that he was sending money to Lorimar every month. She wanted Arthur to be totally dependent on her. They'd even been to a lawyer making her the executrix of his will. He had no family and his friend Ruth Eddleman, who was his executrix before the change, was on sabbatical in England."

"So Annika had been planning this for quite a while?"

"I think she began planning to befriend Jacobs even before she returned here from her job in Connecticut. We found newspaper articles in her room about Arthur coming to South Kingstown. I believe their meeting had nothing at all to do with fate. She rationalized that she was doing all of this to protect Arthur, but it always was about protecting her own interests."

"Nordstrum never mailed the letter?"

"Apparently. When Arthur didn't receive a reply, he asked Nordstrum to take him to the lawyer to give the rights to his book to Lorimar. We think this may be when she started drugging him. She was spending more time at his house making his meals. When his license was eventually taken from him, she had the control she wanted and she made plans to move in full time. He began to talk about going to New York to see Lorimar. Nordstrum had him send off another letter she typed for him. However, after he signed it, she'd added a postscript. In it were arrangements to meet her at the train station and a request she bring the manuscript with her. Lorimar called Annika and confirmed she would be there with the manuscript."

"And that sealed her fate?"

"Yes, it did. At approximately 11:55PM, Annika Nordstrum murdered Dorathea Lorimar by striking her on the head with a rock found at the scene and determined to be the murder weapon."

"And she intended to get away with this by implicating Darnell Sharkey?"

"Exactly. In the months prior to the murder, Nordstrum befriended Darnell Sharkey with the intention of framing him for the crime. On Friday, Mr. Sharkey was brought in for questioning. Subsequently, he was released when alibis were given which corroborated placing him elsewhere at the time the murder was committed.

"Annika had arranged for Darnell Sharkey to meet her at the train station that night, placing him there at the scene of the crime. When she called to tell him she would not be arriving, she thought he would go right home as usual. She'd been planning this for a few months, knowing she would have to make sure he had no alibi for that night.

"On Tuesday morning, Ms. Nordstrum went to the home of Geralynn Sharkey to bring her a prescription for heart medicine. She'd taken Mrs. Sharkey prescriptions on previous occasions but had replaced some of the real pills with placebos. That morning, she informed Mrs. Sharkey that her son, Darnell was going to be arrested for murder. Mrs. Sharkey became upset at the news and had an attack. An unopened bottle of pills was found in the downstairs bathroom cabinet. The one Ms. Nordstrum delivered to Mrs. Sharkey that morning. There were no other containers of this medicine in the house when the police arrived on the scene, suggesting that Ms. Nordstrum did not aid Mrs. Sharkey by giving her pills during her seizure. The motive for this was to ensure that Mrs. Sharkey could not alibi her son who would have been home with her at the time of the murder of Miss Dorathea Lorimar."

"So, Nordstrum was unaware that Darnell had stopped at a bar in town and was seen there at the time of the murder?"

"Yes, had she known about that, it may have saved Geralynn's life."

"That's why she was at the scene when you arrived?"

"She was confident she'd made a fool-proof plan. Annika is nothing, if not smug about her superiority over the rest of us, especially men. She left to go to the office and later that night went in search of

Darnell Sharkey. She knew he was staying at their friend Rusty's house. She'd been to his place many times and Darnell knew her as Annie. He didn't realize she was Annika Nordstrum, the reporter doing the story about him on domestic violence. We believe she may have been planning on killing him, too and making it look like a suicide but she was inadvertently locked in the cellar and unable to carry out the rest of her plan at that time.

"She escaped from the cellar and returned to Mr. Arthur Jacob's residence. When she discovered he wasn't there, she checked the phone messages and realized she had to insure Darnell Sharkey was the prime suspect to stop him from providing evidence as to her role in the killing of Lorimar. She went to Mr. Sharkey's home and placed pills into his tea, setting up the appearance that he'd committed suicide.

"I found him unconscious when I returned to the house to confirm my suspicions about Geralynn's medication. He was treated and provided us with information leading to the arrest of Ms. Nordstrum on Saturday evening at the home of Mr. Jacobs."

"Do you feel you have enough evidence to convict her?"

"Yes, we have evidence that places her at the scene of the crime and we have witnesses who will testify against her. We definitely will get a conviction on the murder of Dorathea Lorimar and the attempted murder of Darnelle Sharkey. It will be a bit more complicated as to her culpability in Geralynn Sharkey's death, but we think we can eventually bring that to trial."

"I was curious about one thing. Why did she take the bicycle that night? Surely she could have parked her car somewhere out of sight and walked to the bike path?"

"Yes, but she really hadn't planned on her car giving her trouble. She'd noticed the tire was flat at the Mews and had it filled across the street before taking her friend Justin home. She didn't have a spare with her, so she drove it to Arthur's and left it in the driveway. She was afraid the tire would deflate again, so she used her friend, Justin's bicycle to go down South Road to the bike path leading to the station. She was seen by a witness coming off the path onto South Road after the murder."

Kara picked up the evidence bag containing the tinsel she had found on the bike path that first day.

"This all seems unbelievably devious. I look at her and see such a beautiful, young woman with everything going for her. And yet, it wasn't enough."

"I've come to realize that in this world there are givers and takers. And sometimes there just never is enough for the takers, Sir."

Thanksgiving Day, November 26

Stewart and Kara arrived early to help Ruth get ready for her Thanksgiving celebration. Samuel was in the dining room adding another leaf to the table. More guests were expected later on. Stewart joined in to help.

Kara went into the kitchen where Ruth was directing Arthur in cutting up vegetables for a salad. Kara started getting out plates and silverware. When Stewart came in to collect them, he gave her a kiss on the back of her neck.

"Oooooh, sweet!" Ruth said and he went over and kissed her on the cheek whispering, "Thanks for doing this, Ruth. Right now we really can use a celebration."

From the dining room they could hear Samuel, "Ruth, we need a longer table cloth out here."

"Look in the bottom drawer of the side table. The ecru embossed should do it."

"Ecru? Is that a vegetable? What's ecru?"

Stewart left to help him.

"So who are all these unexpected guests we'll be sharing a meal with?" Kara asked.

"Arthur invited JayZee and Justin and I have some new friends I want you all to meet."

"And would one of them be your latest beau?"

Ruth answered by handing Kara a paring knife. "Those potatoes aren't going to peel themselves."

"Ah, the old potato peeling ploy. Often used in kitchens to deflect conversation not going in the right direction."

Ruth ignored her, but Arthur glanced up from tossing the salad and winked.

"Arthur, do you know something I don't? You two do realize by now, you can't keep secrets from me?"

Arthur made a gesture of zipping his lip.

"So, that's how it's going to be?"

Ruth gave Arthur a warning look causing him to duck his head down and concentrate on tossing the vegetables.

"You keep that up and you'll turn that salad into veggie puree." Kara's stare was causing him great discomfort.

"That looks great, Arthur. Could you take this silverware out to the table?" Ruth stepped in, giving him a chance to escape from the room.

"He seems to be doing much better. I saw him in town the other day at Belmont's. He was talking to some people in the parking lot and they were laughing. It's good to see him out and about."

"He still calls me late at night. I think it's going to take a long time for him to get over Thea's death and Neeka's betrayal. But on a positive note, he has agreed to come speak with my class about his book."

"That's an important move toward healing. Has he decided what he's going to do about the 50th Anniversary?"

"Yes, he's been working with the university to set up a special endowment in Thea's name and he's written a lovely inscription for the Anniversary Addition."

"How are you doing with her notebooks?"

"I'm putting all her work together in a special collection and establishing a Dorathea Lorimar Foundation. We'll use the proceeds from the sale to offer scholarships for promising authors. It should be published by next summer," Ruth told her. They stopped the conversation when Arthur returned.

"A car just pulled up outside. I think JayZee and Justin are here." Ruth went to the front door to greet her guests.

"Arthur, Ruth was just telling me about the plans you've been making for the anniversary of your book.'

"I still think of it as Thea's book. I believe she'd approve of what we're doing. I'll make sure she's never forgotten. I just wish I could have helped her more when…" He didn't finish the sentence. "Would you like to see the inscription for the new edition?" He took a folded sheet of paper from his back pocket and gave it to her. His hand was shaking. Kara unfolded it and silently read his words.

I lovingly dedicate this book to my friend Miss Dorathea Lorimar. Without her constant encouragement, invaluable support, undaunting loyalty and fine writing and editing skills, A Quiet Death would never have been written. It is as much her book as it has been mine for all of these fifty years.

Arthur Jacobs

"That's beautiful, Arthur. I know Thea would approve." She returned it to him just as JayZee and Justin came into the kitchen with their arms full of boxes.

"Homemade pies from Schartner's Farm. Apple, pecan and pumpkin."

"And we didn't forget you, Arthur. A lemon-meringue pie from Gregg's." Justin put the box on the table.

"What can we do to help?"

"There are glasses in the hutch out there. If you could put them on the table and find out what people are drinking."

An hour later, everyone was sitting around the living room. The Macy's Parade had ended, Santa had arrived and the smell of turkey permeated the house. The doorbell rang and Ruth rushed to answer it.

Three people crowded into the foyer enthusiastically talking all at once. Arthur went to collect their coats and hang them in the hall closet. Ruth walked into the living room with her guests.

"Everyone, I'd like you to meet the Carnavale family: Sophia, Gino and Rick." Sophia smiled and nodded as Gino went from person to person, enthusiastically shaking hands. "Nice ta meetcha. Good ta meetcha, Great to be heeyah."

Rick stood with his arm around a grinning Ruth. "Everyone, I'd like you to meet my good friend, Rick Carnavale." They both smiled as Ruth added, "Known to some of us here as 'Chatty Cathy'." She looked over at Kara who came forward and held out her hand. Rick grabbed her into a big bear hug and when he finally released her, Ruth announced, "Dinner is now being served."

❧

Epilogue

The following August, on a night when the Perseids Meteor Showers graced the sky above Kingston, a memorial service was held at the Congregational Church for Dorathea Lorimar.

With the stars showering down from overhead, friends carried her remains to a quiet spot along the ocean. Casting them on to the white-capped waves hugging the rocks, her ashes gently floated on the tips of the waves along the shore, melding with the sand and the sea. It was, finally, a peaceful end to a quiet life.

About South County

Show me a great setting and I'll write you a story. Certain places inspire me and from the first time I arrived in South Kingstown, I've been in love with this area in the southern part of our small state.

I attended the University of Rhode Island and after graduating, decided to settle here in South County. I've watched it grow over the past fifty years. There was a time, back in the day, that the only place you could get breakfast was at the local bowling alley. Or you could arrive early and stand in line outside Phil's hoping to get inside before it closed for the afternoon. Today, restaurants, homes and businesses have sprung up everywhere. And the once tiny, agricultural campus has never stopped growing with it. But that little stretch of village just outside the university's main entrance has somehow managed to retain its historic beginnings.

Now, you should understand that South County is the name given to it by the locals. You'll not find it on the map because it is, in actuality, Washington County. Originally it was King's County, but in 1781 was renamed Washington County in honor of the General/President after he stopped over in "Little Rest" (Kingston) on his way to Newport in March of that year. According to *Washington's Travels in New England*, which Charles Eugene Claghorn III based on Washington's diary entries, he and his aide, Alexander Hamilton, ate dinner at Mr. Kenyon's tavern and lodged that night at the tavern owned by Lieutenant Ichabod Potter, Jr.

In *Last Train to Kingston*, Arthur Jacobs, a Pulitzer Prize winning author, is asked to speak at the college's writers' conference. He falls in love with the village and, like me, he decides to stay. Kingston's walkways, stonewalls and historic buildings comprise Jacob's neighborhood. He buys the B.F. Brown Mansard House(c.1875) and often wanders the bricked sidewalks, visiting with the people who reside and work in the village. The plaques on each building speak to the history within their walls.

Arthur is a regular at Fayerweather House. This cottage was built in 1820 by the town's blacksmith, George Fayerweather, next to his business, which served as the town's blacksmith shop for the better part of the 19th Century. It's a favorite haunt of mine, as I belong to the Fayerweather Craft Guild and work with fellow crafters selling our hand-made products in the rooms, which were restored after being purchased by the Kingston Improvement Association in 1962. Our website is www.fayerweatherhouse.com

I travel through the village almost every day and have spent countless hours inside the Kingston Free Library, once the old courthouse. Besides checking out books, I've rehearsed and performed in a community theatre production on the library's second floor and have recently strummed my ukulele with other uke enthusiasts in that same room.

Rainy days can be passed pleasantly perusing the antique prints and books at the Kingston Hill Store (1850) and on Sunday mornings you usually can find me attending services at the Kingston Congregational Church (1820).

In my younger years I spent a summer college semester living in a second-floor room at the inn next door to the church. My father thought the 1757 on the Kingston Inn sign out front was the address but soon realized from the sloping wood floors and the flaking plaster on the stairs, that 1757 was the date when the building was constructed. He brought me outside and walked me around the inn, pointing out the fire escapes and shaking his head all the while. I have a rich history of my own with this little village.

Of course, I must mention the Courthouse Center for the Arts, courthousearts.org It housed the county's third courthouse back in 1892. Upon construction of a more modern structure, the building became empty and in the 1990's refashioned itself into a performance/art center. This is where we first meet the Carnivale brothers, Gino and Rick. Gino is the custodian and his brother Rick drives the local taxi service to and from the railway station. On a night in late November, they become embroiled in a murder which had taken place on the bike path adjacent to the nearby tracks.

The railway station is where I'll end my little tour of some of the historic settings in this book. I've stood many times on the platform like Thea Lorimar did on the last night of her life. And I've taken the train on occasion from Kingston north to Boston and south to Penn

Station just as Detective Kara Langley does on her trip to New York to investigate Lorimar's death. It has changed a bit over the years, adding an over-the-rails walkway and new tracks for faster trains. The 1875 Victorian clapboard structure is a small wonder to view from the bridge on Route 138. I look down on it every day as I travel from my home to the University or on my way into town and I couldn't think of a better place to set the opening for my first hometown mystery.

For those wanting to know more about the history, people, architecture and other interesting SC facts, here are some resources:

RI Historical Preservation Commission. "State of Rhode Island and Providence Plantations Preliminary Survey Report Town of South Kingstown." Providence: Rhode Island Historical Preservation Commission, 1984.

McBurney, Christian M. *A History of Kingston, RI*, 1700-1900, Heart of Rural South County. Pettaquamscutt Historical Society, Kingston, RI, 2004.

And if you're ever in the area, you could plan a visit to the South County History Center at 2636 Kingstown Road right in the center of the Village.

www.southcountyhistorycenter.org

Index of Photographs

Acknowledgments

Special thanks to Michael Grossman, Robert Benjamin, Zack Perry, Tracy Heffron, Detective Jennifer Natale of the South Kingstown Police Department, and Alicia Vaandering of the South County History Center.

About the Author

Claremary Sweeney is a writer/photographer living in South Kingstown, Rhode Island. She spent her earlier years in the field of education and now, retired, uses her imagination to create stories that can be enjoyed by children of all ages and the young at heart. Within *A Berkshire Tale*, are the original ten ZuZu Stories about the adventures of a kitten born on a farm in the Berkshire Hills. The book is filled with the settings that make this area an historic as well as a cultural center in western Massachusetts. She continues to write other tales in this series and is currently working on a Christmas adventure set in Stockbridge during the annual Norman Rockwell Weekend held during the first week of December each year.

Last Train to Kingston is the first in a series of adult mysteries using Rhode Island historical sites. *Last Rose on the Vine* and *Last Carol of the Season* are the next books in this series.

The author lives with her husband Charley and their two cats ZuZu and Roxie. Roxie hopes, some day, to have a book of her own, but for now spends time complaining about being "Roxie Dammit, aka The Other Cat" in featured posts on Ms. Sweeney's blog, *Around ZuZu's Barn, Conversations With Kindred Spirits* at www.aroundzuzusbarn.com

OTHER BOOKS BY CLAREMARY SWEENEY

A Berkshire Tale is made up of ten interconnected stories set in the

ıusetts. The tales center around ZuZu, a tabby kitten born in a barn at Tanglewood, the summer home of the Boston Symphony Orchestra. From the kitten's first experience with Mozart, to her friendship with Nick and their adventures at some of the many famous places around Lenox, adults and children will find these stories charming and educational.

The Pacas Are Coming! ZuZu and the Crias The January story from

A Berkshire Tale has been developed into a larger version of the original tale with additional illustrations. ZuZu finds herself with a serious case of "cabin fever" having been snowed in the barn for weeks. She is worried winter will never end, but one day, she hears that new animals soon will be arriving - animals that hum and have beautiful fleece. She can't wait to meet these gentle creatures and runs to her Mama with the news that "The pacas are coming! The pacas are coming!" And so begins her adventures with the alpaca crias, Ginger and Twyla on their farm in the beautiful Hills of the Berkshires.

Carnivore Conundrum One morning, Adonis, a baby pitcher plant,

awakes to find a fly flailing around in his digestive juices. The fly begs for its life and Adonis spits it out vowing never to eat meat again. This causes much consternation for his mother. As she pleads with her baby and frets the hours away, the other plants and wildlife in the glass house try to find a solution to this vexing problem.

Carnivore Conundrum is a book in verse set at the Roger Williams Park Botanical Gardens in Providence, Rhode Island and is illustrated by Zack Perry, a student at the University of Rhode Island.

Ms. Sweeney is presently working on ***A Christmas Tale - ZuZu's Homecoming***, set in Stockbridge, Massachusetts during the Norman Rockwell Weekend held the first week in December each year.

Last Rose on the Vine - The body of Professor Paul Waddington is found in the University of Rhode Island's rose garden. His throat is slashed and a Rhode Island Red Rose is tucked into his lapel. Detective Lieutenant Kara Langley searches for leads, unearthing allegations of harassment and embezzlement in the victim's past. Kara must sift through clues to find the murderer among a motley group of potential killers.

Last Carol of the Season - Detective Lieutenant Kara Langley is enjoying Black Friday with her friends, Ruth Eddleman and Sophia Carnavale when their shopping spree is abruptly interrupted. The body of Sherman Pruitt is discovered in the dressing room of Main Street's historic Kenyon's Department Store. Kara recognizes the victim from a domestic violence call during her earlier years on the police force. The Holiday Season in Wakefield turns sinister when Kara and Detective Carl Sullivan investigate the murder of a very unpopular man.